A *L*INE UNSUNDERED

A GODWORLDS NOVELLA

R. M. SMITH

Dedicated to Tommi,

Who has never stopped encouraging me throughout all my dramas, crazy ideas and wild dreams.

CONTENTS

ACKNOWLEDGEMENTS

It goes without saying that I owe the publication of this book to some key people, without whom I'd still be battling with a very immature manuscript.

Firstly, to my friend Jonny, who persisted with the drafts I sent him and taught me much of what I know now about writing fiction. Without you my friend, this would certainly be a very different piece of work.

Secondly, to my friend Tori, who scoured the manuscript for spelling and grammar errors alongside her own job as a professional article writer for The Islander, a local magazine in Mallorca. Also to Connor, who did the same despite his own misgivings about being able to spot mistakes.

Thirdly, to Daniel Hasenbos, who took my basic, amateur drawings and transformed them into the beautiful map and family tree you see at the front of this book. Check out danielsmaps.com for more of his great work.

Finally, to the lovely group of ladies who helped me to understand how a mother feels about their child – something I can never appreciate. Your insight and feedback inspired the development of two of the most important characters.

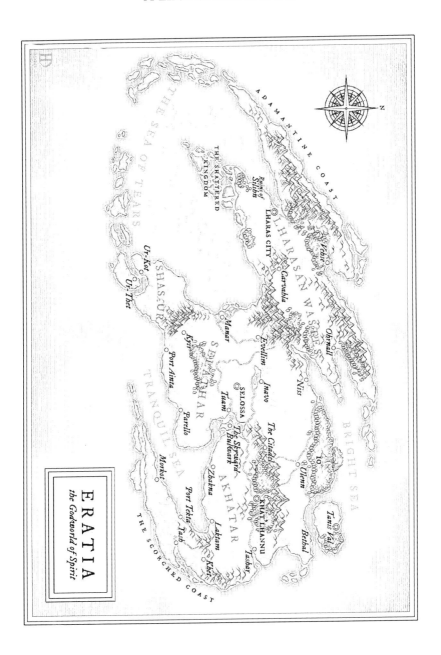

ERATIA
the Godsworld of Spirit

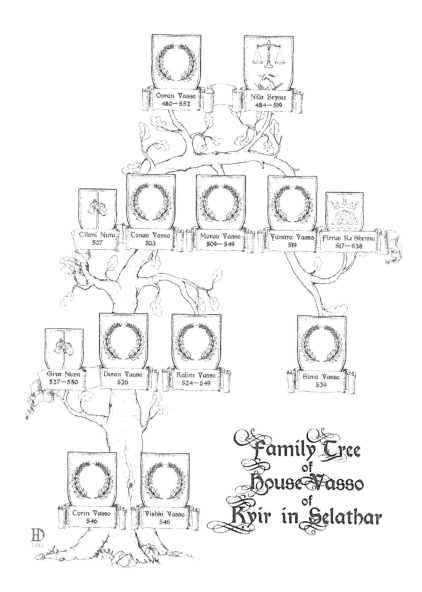

Family Tree
of
House Vasso
of
Kyir in Selathar

PROLOGUE

THE SETTING SUN cast striking bands of pink and red across the sky as Imdan Talet surveyed the misty green marshlands over which he held lordship. Groups of ramshackle wooden houses sat on stilts above the waterline, connected by aging log walkways and rope bridges. The townsfolk milled about as they returned to their homes for the evening, laughing and joking in their usual high spirits. Manar was not the wealthiest of the Selathi provinces, but the people maintained a quiet joy in the simplicity of their lives.

"So, what do you think Father?" Naidar asked eagerly.

Clenching his jaw, Imdan turned to face his son who was frantically wringing his hands a few feet away. The candlelight illuminated his nervous expression, and the sight of Naidar's weak face made Imdan sneer. *Look at that weak face. Weak chin. Timid eyes. Eratia knows how you could ever be of my blood.*

"As usual, I am unsurprised by your inability to comprehend the consequences of your actions. Despite everything I have taught you, all the lessons, the chidings, the beatings, none of it has sunk into that thick skull of yours."

He approached the table and poured himself a cup of wine. Naidar moved to do the same, but a menacing glare from Imdan caused him to retreat.

"What you propose is tantamount to suicide for our House,"

Imdan continued, taking a sip from his cup. "The Paragon exists to deter exactly the kind of treachery you are getting yourself involved in. He will not allow it to go unpunished."

"Only if we are discovered, Father!" Naidar exclaimed. "My associate has assured me that we can carry out the plan without anyone finding out the truth."

Imdan slammed his hand down on the table, causing the wine jug to rattle on its tray.

"You are talking about overthrowing another House!" he shouted, before pausing to lower his voice. It would not do to have a spy overhearing their conversation. "Placing a puppet in the seat and ruling their lands by proxy! Such an action would ripple throughout Selathar and draw the scrutiny of every Houselord from here to Bethal. It would bring the retribution of the Paragon and his army straight down on top of us. You cannot keep something like this hidden, not from him. The peace and prosperity that I have worked so hard to build could be undone in a single night, do you understand that?"

His ancestors would have balked at the state that House Talet was in when Imdan had assumed the mantle of Houselord. Years of weak leadership by his father and grandfather had left it on the brink of collapse, but his firm and decisive approach to lordship had saved both the House and the people of Manar from starvation and ruin. The other Houselords had expected a I, brash young man to enter the political scene, one they could manipulate into a position more suited to their schemes.

They had been surprised and not a little disappointed to discover that Imdan was not his father's son. He had learned quickly that nobody could be trusted, and several early assassination attempts had honed him into a suspicious man. He was nonetheless intelligent and ruthless in his dealings with his fellow Houselords, and was known across Selathar as a man who did not suffer fools gladly.

"My lords, if I might offer a word of advice?"

The voice came from the corner of the room. Javin Kassar, his personal advisor, was stood in the doorway. Similar in age to Imdan himself, he had been in service to House Talet for only five years, but had already demonstrated a fierce loyalty to their family. He had taken over in attempting to teach Naidar the fundamentals of lordship, which had removed the burden from Imdan.

Small mercies, he thought, gesturing for Javin to enter.

"Thank you, my lord," Javin said with a bow. He walked over to where they stood and placed a hand on Naidar's shoulder.

"Strange as this may sound, I find myself agreeing with the young lord," he said.

"I never found your twisted sense of humour particularly funny, Javin," Imdan retorted. "You cannot seriously think this plan of his has merit? The chances of something going wrong are far greater than him achieving success here."

Imdan's shrewd attitude towards others did not exclude members of his own family, particularly his firstborn son Naidar. The boy displayed all the characteristics that Imdan despised; he was headstrong, tactless, and excitable to the point of immaturity. He showed none of the subtlety and diplomatic flair that Imdan possessed, and he frequently embarrassed both himself and the House in front of others.

Once, he had begged to be given the chance to receive a visiting Houselord at the gates to their manor. Upon seeing a woman in a rough travel cloak dismounting her horse in the gatehouse, he had demanded she move along as 'more important visitors' were on their way. Lady Jamma of House Somur was on her horse and nearly back through the gate to Evellim before Imdan had caught up to her. The beating he gave Naidar that night left the boy unconscious for three days, though he had no regrets. The boy had to learn.

Not that any of Imdan's lessons tempered Naidar's reckless enthusiasm. His latest scheme was proof that some words fell on deaf ears.

Javin chuckled and placed his hands behind his back.

"With the right guidance, I believe this ambitious plan can be executed without our part in it being exposed. There is much to gain here, my lord, and with proper mitigation of the risks I believe it will succeed."

"And if he fails?" Imdan demanded, pointing at Naidar. "House Talet will not survive the judgment of the Paragon, Javin. Even if Rannad came to me with this plan, I would be loathe to allow it."

Rannad was his secondborn son, and frankly was everything Naidar was not. Imdan had long wished that they had been born the other way round, so that Rannad would succeed him as

Houselord. Their laws forbade an heir to be passed over, however, even by their own choice. Only death or imprisonment could shift the line of succession to the next child.

Only death. Or imprisonment.

Naidar stepped forward. "Please Father, let me do this. I'll take Javin with me for counsel. With him there to advise me, we can secure our House's rightful place in Selathi politics for generations to come."

Imdan turned away from them and returned to the window. The sun had now set, leaving a dark red haze in the sky as night approached. The dusklarks were deep into their evening songs, and the town below was only visible by the many torches that cut through the darkness.

Javin was a wise man, with extensive knowledge of every ruling House in Selathar. If he believed the plan could succeed then it likely would, so long as Naidar did as he was told.

The prospect of unchallenged influence over the southwestern Provinces sparked a flame of ambition in Imdan's heart. He had always possessed a desire for more power, but he was careful to check his impulses. Only foolish men allowed their dreams to control them, and the wrong move could seal House Talet's fate.

The risk had to be worth the rewards. Imdan preferred guarantees, if not by chance then of his own making. If the plan succeeded, they would secretly command wealth and influence amongst the other Houses at a level unseen since before the Province Wars. If it failed, and they were discovered, they would disappear into history as traitors and thieves. Imdan had to make the potential failure less extreme, less costly.

If he couldn't ensure success, then he could at least limit the potential loss. He could ensure that House Talet would at least have a future.

For that, Naidar would have to die.

Any blame could be placed on him, and Rannad would become his heir, just as he always should have been.

Sacrifices must be made, he reminded himself.

"Javin, listen well," he said quietly, not moving from the window. "The boy is your responsibility. If I allow this, it is on the understanding that you are responsible for tempering his reckless tongue. If anything goes wrong, you will pay the price along with him. Do I make myself clear?"

Bowing his head, Javin maintained a sombre expression. "Absolutely, my lord. The young lord and I have been speaking at length about his...spirited attitude, and I believe he can be entrusted with this opportunity. I will accompany him, however, at your request."

Imdan looked at Naidar, a momentary sensation of regret creeping into his heart. Pushing it away, he walked over and placed a hand on his shoulder. "I have not always been a kind father to you. It has been for your own good, to prepare you for your time as Houselord. This is your final opportunity to prove yourself to me, and your final test. If you pass, I will consider you the son you have always longed to be. If you fail, you will not be alive to dwell on it. Do we understand one another?"

Naidar looked at him, the expression on his face a mixture of pride and fear. "Yes Father," he replied quietly.

"Then send your response. You will depart as soon as the invitation to negotiate is received from our friends to the south."

Smiling weakly, Naidar turned and left the room.

Javin made to follow him, but stopped in the doorway. "My lord," he asked, a puzzled look on his face, "if I may ask, why the change of heart?"

"You are my advisor Javin," Imdan replied, "and I am a Houselord. It is a poor lord who does not take advice when it is justified."

Javin smiled and exited the room, leaving Imdan alone to sip his wine in silence.

Yes, he thought, *sacrifices must be made.*

* * *

IT WAS A small group that left Manar on a crisp morning some weeks later, banners flapping in the dawn breeze. Some twenty retainers accompanied Naidar Talet on his journey south, consisting of a cohort of soldiers for protection as well as attendants, musicians and his own personal herald.

His hubris is truly staggering.

Imdan stood atop the battlements, observing his son's departure with a stony expression on his face. As Naidar crossed the moat bridge, he turned and offered his father a salute, striking his fist across his chest. Imdan returned the salute, though it was a token offering at best.

As he watched the group proceed along the south road, he felt the hairs on the back of his neck stand on end. A cold sensation crept through his body, and Imdan steeled himself as he turned to regard the figure emerging from the shadows of the gatehouse tower.

Hunched over and draped in dirty black robes, it knelt in front of him and looked into his eyes. At least, that was how it felt to Imdan. There was no face visible under the hood of the robes, and he could barely stand to look at the creature.

"You summoned me," came a voice like gravel.

Suppressing a shudder, Imdan turned to look at Naidar's retinue approaching a hill in the distance. "You understand what is required of you?"

Though he could not see the creature's face, he could feel its gaze upon him. It pierced him like a dagger of ice, intensifying the cold feeling in his body. "I do," it replied, bowing its head slightly.

"Good. Now get out of my sight."

The creature withdrew into the shadows, as though it was never there.

Imdan watched as Naidar's group disappeared over the hill and towards the mountains in the south.

"Goodbye, my son."

CHAPTER ONE

TONAS VASSO SAT by his father's bedside, watching as the lord of their House and ruler of Kyir struggled to breathe through his final moments. Death had come for Osran Vasso after a long and fulfilling life, though that was small comfort for Tonas as he struggled to come to terms with the thought of losing his father.

The old lord lay on his deathbed, his eyes heavy and breath shallow. Soft, white pillows supported his fragile head, and silk sheets were draped over his aged body like funeral muslin. The window was open, allowing a cool, spring breeze to enter the room and dance across his face. Tonas knew he couldn't feel it – the illness had robbed Osran of the sense of touch some months previously. He would be able to smell it, however. The scent of grass, flowers, and freshly tilled earth would tell his father that the seasonal harvest was well underway.

Osran was one of the most respected and influential Houselords in Selathar, and under normal circumstances word of his impending death would have been sent to the other Houses so that they might send a son or daughter to offer their condolences. Impending political intrigue, however, meant that this had been discounted some weeks ago. The fewer Houses that were involved in the upcoming talks, the better.

This was a time for family, and only Osran's closest kin were permitted to be in his chamber at the time of his passing. Tonas was his firstborn son and heir to the lordship of House Vasso. Approaching his fiftieth year, he was a stern man who took his role as the future Houselord very seriously.

His wife Ciloni was stood behind him, her hand on his shoulder for comfort whilst maintaining a respectful distance. Whilst she was the mother of his children, Tonas knew she acknowledged the fact that she was not a Vasso by birth. Blood ties were extremely important to their House, and those not of Vasso lineage were not afforded any rights of succession or inheritance.

Osran coughed suddenly, and Tonas gently grasped his hand.

"How do you feel, father?" he asked softly. "Is there any pain?"

The old man turned to look at him, a movement that seemed to take a great deal of effort. "No pain, my son. I'm just...tired. I suppose I should be grateful for a peaceful death." He smiled, and Tonas saw his eyelids drop.

"Father, stay with us. We can postpone the negotiations until you are better. I can't lead them without your counsel." A tear rolled down Tonas' cheek, and he wiped it away in embarrassment. He knew his words were futile, almost bordering on denial, but he couldn't help it. He still held some semblance of hope that Osran would recover.

"The negotiations must continue, my son," Osran replied with a reassuring tone. "To call them off now would risk insulting another Houselord and calling our family's honour into question. My life is not so important that we can risk such a thing. I have faith that you will do me proud. You have the temperament and wisdom to lead our House, and a strong family to support you."

A snort of derision came from the window, and Tonas looked up sharply for the source of the noise with a disapproving look in his eyes.

His sister Yanara was leant casually against the wall by the window, her arms folded across her chest and wearing a decidedly imperious expression on her face. Her demeanour was borderline disrespectful, though not so much as the fact she had her rapier strapped to her waist.

That damned weapon, Tonas thought. *Why Father let her keep it, I'll never know.*

Whilst an attractive woman, her insistence on wearing dark

leather jerkins and riding pants combined with her unnatural white hair and grey eyes meant that the rapier was simply the finishing touch to Yanara's decidedly rebellious attire. When Osran had ordered her to stop wearing it, she had responded by slashing half the paintings in the Great Hall until he relented. No one had dared questioned her since.

Tonas' expression was stern as he addressed her. "What was that noise for, Yanara? And how dare you bring that weapon in here, of all places? I can't believe you would continue to disrespect Father even as he lays here on his deathbed!" The last few words were a shout, and it wasn't until Ciloni squeezed his shoulder that he realized he was leaning forward with his hands clenched.

Sighing, he sat back in the chair and looked at his sister with disappointed eyes. They had never been particularly close, even as children. Considering the fourteen year age gap and the fact that Tonas had spent most of his adolescent years studying to succeed his father, there simply hadn't been the time. It was his younger brother Moras who had been the brother Yanara had deserved, and they had been very close when they were younger.

In recent years she had become increasingly difficult, often refusing to assist in family business and striking out to conduct business on her own initiative. Sometimes it benefitted the House, other times it didn't. One could never tell with Yanara these days.

"Brother, you of all people know what this weapon represents," she snarled at him. "Don't pretend this is about anything other than your discomfort with it. I don't ask for much, least of all from you, but I won't permit you to lecture me about respect and honour!"

Tonas clenched his jaw. She was right, of course, when she said he was uncomfortable with her wearing the rapier. It had belonged to another man once, many years ago. He knew what it meant to her, and he knew what she meant by wearing it, especially now. It was her way of honouring a memory, and at the same time dishonouring him and Osran.

He opened his mouth to reply, but the elder Vasso squeezed his hand.

"Please," Osran croaked, "must you fight even now? At least let me pretend that my children love one another, just for a moment. After I'm gone, you can bicker to your hearts' content."

Yanara sighed and walked over to the bed, placing a hand on

Osran's arm. "As you wish, old man." She paused for a moment, before putting on a forced smile. "I mean, *Father*."

Tonas was stunned. Yanara hadn't used that word in front of Osran in over ten years, refusing to acknowledge their relationship. He doubted her sincerity, but the effect on Osran was the same.

Tears welled up in his eyes, and he broke into a weak smile. "Thank you, my daughter," he said. "I know I have not always been a good father to you, but you have become a strong and capable woman nonetheless. I regret much of what has happened between us in the past, but I know there is nothing I can do or say to change any of it."

Yanara simply nodded, and returned to her position by the window, choosing now to look out onto the fields rather than face the rest of the room. Tonas couldn't help but wonder how she would behave now that she was facing the prospect of being sister to the Houselord.

She had organised the upcoming negotiations, however, which went some way to allaying his doubts. Yanara had spent months in talks with her contact just to convince them to attend the negotiations. Perhaps she was finally learning to reconcile the past with the present.

The feeling of Osran's hand on his own brought Tonas' attention back to reality.

"My son, you have grown into a fine man," the elder Vasso said weakly. "You have proven yourself a loyal son, and a devoted father and grandfather. You have difficult times ahead, not only in representing our House in negotiations, but also in learning what it means to lead. I am not worried, though, for I have faith that under your Lordship, House Vasso will continue to prosper and flourish. A man could not hope for a better heir, or a better son. Knowing you are here to rule after me, I can finally rest."

And then, as if timed to the second, Osran's breath suddenly grew short, then stopped altogether as his eyelids fluttered shut and he slipped away.

Silence hung over the room, broken only by the sound of Ciloni weeping. Tonas bowed his head in grief, but did not shed tears as his wife did. It was important for him to be strong now, not only for his House but also for the people of Kyir. He looked to the window, hoping to see any kind of reaction from Yanara, but she continued to stare out of the window. He thought he saw her shoulders relax slightly, but assumed it was simply her breathing.

He rose from his seat and turned to his Ciloni, embracing his wife for a moment. When they broke apart, he smiled at her weakly.

"Well, he's gone. We should start making arrangements for the funeral. We need to ensure that the appropriate invitations are sent, and the people of Kyir must be informed."

"My love," Ciloni interjected, "you have other things to take care of. For now, why don't you let me take care of all the small details and take some of the burden off you?"

Tonas smiled at her and kissed her on the cheek. Her love and support were important to him, and she would likely be his crutch in the coming days and weeks.

Turning to Yanara, he cleared his throat. "Sister, would you inform the children? I need to stay and wait for the Sisters to perform the Rite of Passing." She remained at the window, as though she hadn't heard him. "Yanara, now," he said with a commanding tone.

She turned from the window and regarded him with a defiant expression on her face. For a moment, Tonas thought she was about to refuse him. Amongst everything else going on, the last thing he needed was for her to begin resisting his authority as the new Houselord.

But her expression softened, and she offered him a slight bow.

"As you say, brother. I mean, *my lord.*" She finished with the same tone she had used when addressing Osran as 'Father', as though she were offering him a token gift.

Moving away from the window, Yanara walked around the edge of the room towards the door, seemingly keeping her distance from both the bed and Tonas. He turned to his wife and nodded. "My love, why don't you go as well?" he said softly. "I would appreciate some time alone with my thoughts before the Sisters arrive."

Ciloni bowed and left the room, with Yanara following shortly behind her. A few seconds later Tonas was stood alone in the Houselord's chambers, with his father's body laid on the bed.

He walked over to the window where Yanara had been stood and gazed out over the vast fields below. Vasso Keep, their ancestral home, sat atop a great hill which afforded a commanding view of the surrounding countryside. The farmers were busy harvesting the wheat with support from the local townsfolk, a job which everyone took to with enthusiasm. As he would have to do himself in the days to come.

Am I ready for this, Father? Were you?

He wept quietly, glad that nobody was around to see his tears.

* * *

THE SISTERS TOOK great care in the preparation of Osran's body. Working quickly but delicately, they applied the necessary lotions and embalming fluids before wrapping him in the funeral shroud of the House. The silk shroud had been used for over two hundred years, and was removed and cleansed prior to the burial of every Houselord in the Vasso line.

The Order of Luminous Sisters belonged to the Selathi religion, Erati Sel. Responsible for preparing dying Selai for their next journeys after death, they were headquartered at the temple known as the Skyward Bulwark, though there were localized chapters in almost every Selathi town. The Bulwark sat on a large island located at the head of the Tranquil Sea between Selathar and Akhatar, making it a natural stopping point for those travelling between the two nations. Osran himself had stopped there on several occasions during his trade missions to Akhatar, and found a peace in their teachings. As the years had passed, he had become more and more spiritual, especially as he approached his final days.

Tonas stood in the doorway, watching as they laboured. Whilst not a devout follower of Erati Sel, he respected the fact that his father had been. His own job during the Rite was to guard the room against intruders, as was the traditional duty of the heir whenever a Vasso lord passed away. It would not be his last duty, however.

Difficult times were ahead, not least the prospect of negotiating with the firstborn son of another House. Whilst the Paragon kept the peace between the Houses of Selathar, the old rivalries could not be easily brushed aside.

House Vasso had controlled the south western approaches to the nation of Shas-Ur for the last one hundred years, ever since the end of the Last Realm War. At that time, the sheer loss of life and devastation caused by the constant fighting had left most Houses on the verge of collapse. With most of their forces gone and unable to defend their territories, it had left them all vulnerable to outside aggressors. Eventually, repeated attacks by foreign raiders united the Houses and formed their Houselords into the first Selathi Council.

The Council was kept in check by the Paragons of Selathar. Successive leaders who commanded a substantial peacekeeping army, they were stripped of all ambition and desire by the mysterious Vault Masters of Selossa. Raised both to lead and to serve, they ensured that the Houses remained at peace and didn't descend back into territorial fighting or open warfare. There were still disputes between Houselords that required resolving, but the days of settling their differences through local wars were long gone. Tensions could still run high, however, especially in the western towns where the ravages of Lharasan raids were still being felt.

Tonas would have to contend with such tension during tomorrow's negotiations, especially as their visitors were expecting to deal with Osran. His father's unexpected death would leave them on edge, and combined with his own misgivings about being unprepared for such a meeting, there was every chance things could go disastrously wrong.

But wasn't this what it meant to lead a House? Risks had to be taken, or stagnation would set in. If they didn't keep moving forward, they would be left behind as the other Houses grew and prospered. Their voice in the Council would be drowned out by those more powerful, and the troubles of House Vasso would only grow.

Their visitors would know this as well. After all, their House would have the same concerns, the same worries as he did. He had to rise to the challenge, or he would set the tone for the rest of his Lordship.

It was time for Tonas to rule.

CHAPTER TWO

Twenty-seven years ago

OSRAN WATCHED WITH a smile as his two youngest children chased each other around the courtyard. Yanara was giggling furiously as she ran from her older brother, Moras. Every time she turned around to see where he was, he would nearly catch her and another fit of giggles would erupt from her little lungs before she shot off again.

Moras was ten years older than Yanara, having just celebrated his sixteenth birthday. With her being only six, Osran noticed that his son had become fiercely protective of her as they had grown older. It was rare that Moras went anywhere without her trailing him, to the point where she had to be taken away when it was time for his more physical instruction. Ladies did not learn to fence or ride.

His thoughts were interrupted by Yanara tripping over the hem of her silk dress and landing face first in the grass. It was a crisp spring morning, and the lawn was still wet with dew. Osran started towards her, but Moras was there in an instant to pick her up. Her dress was now stained with grass and mud, as was her little face, but she was grinning from ear to ear as though it were nothing.

"Look at you," Moras was saying as he brushed her down. "You've gotten your dress all dirty, you little rascal."

"Your fault," Yanara giggled, "You chased me."

They were wonderful children, Osran thought as they continued playing. Whilst Tonas spent his days studying to succeed him, as was his duty, his other son and daughter had no immediate obligations. Of course, Moras understood this more than Yanara did, at least for now. She was still young, and Osran was content to allow her to enjoy her youth whilst it lasted.

Moras would have to accept some responsibilities, however. Whilst not his firstborn and therefore not his direct heir, Osran was a practical man. He knew Tonas would need his brother's support when he became Houselord, though he had to admit he was unsure what form that support would take.

Despite the smaller age gap of six years, Moras was not as close with Tonas as he was with Yanara, something which Osran attributed to the time Tonas spent away from Moras focusing on his studies and his new family. Moras had always kept to himself, and Osran had been concerned that his son was struggling with loneliness until Yanara had been born.

"You look lost in thought, my lord."

Osran turned to see Tonas' wife Ciloni approaching him, with their infant son Kalim swaddled in a blanket in her arms. Less than a year old, this boy would one day succeed Tonas, as Tonas would succeed Osran.

"Ciloni, my dear," Osran said warmly, planting a kiss on her cheek. "How are you? And how is my favourite grandson?"

"You mean your *only* grandson, my lord. Unless you have another one you've done away with somewhere?"

Osran laughed. Ciloni was a sweet girl, but had an exceptionally dry sense of humour. It was one of the reasons he liked her, as it meant she had the wit and intellect to keep Tonas on his toes.

"If I had, I'm sure you'd be the first to figure it out my dear," he chuckled, stroking the infant Kalim's cheek with one finger. "Is Tonas spending enough time with the two of you?"

"As much as he can. I know he's busy," Ciloni replied, shrugging her shoulders slightly.

"Busy learning to lead a House, which includes placing family above all else. I will speak with him."

"Thank you, my lord." Ciloni smiled at him, then nodded towards Moras and Yanara, who were now play fighting on the grass. "They certainly seem to be having fun."

Osran sighed, then shook his head. "I know. I can tell she's going to be a difficult one. She already hates being made to wear dresses, and her governess has to pry her away from Moras whenever it's time for her lessons. I dread the day I have to tell her she needs to marry."

Ciloni laughed. "I wish you luck, my lord. Given how assertive she is already, you might struggle convincing her to go along with that idea."

"Sister!" Ciloni's laugh had echoed across the courtyard and caught Yanara's attention, who was presently sat atop Moras hitting him with a small stick. "Father!" she shouted with glee as she jumped up and ran towards them. "Catch me!"

He managed to scoop her up in his arms as she made a beeline for his midriff, holding her against him and making a soft growling sound as he pretended to bite at her neck. She squealed in mock terror and pushed his face away with her hands.

"No, Father! Don't eat me!" She giggled as she looked him in the eye, her hazel eyes wide with excitement. She was a beautiful child, so full of life and love.

Just like her mother.

Osran felt a jolt of pain as he remembered his wife. Nila had been an incredible woman, more than he deserved. They had met when Osran had been accompanying his own father, Isarl, to trade negotiations in Tuam. Ruled by House Brysee, Tuam was more of a vast collection of docks and wharfs than anything one might reasonably consider a city. However, its position at the head of the Tranquil Sea across from Akhatar made it a hub of trade in the region.

When Houselord Brysee had introduced his daughter to them at dinner, Osran had fallen in love with her instantly. Short but beautiful, with golden hair and dazzling blue eyes, Nila was like the women Osran had pictured in his daydreams. A proposal had followed soon after, and before long the birth of Tonas. Moras' birth came a few years later, and for the decade that followed Osran and Nila had watched as their two sons grew into fine young men. Osran knew, however, that Nila longed for a daughter.

In time, her wish was granted, though it had changed everything. There had been no signs of complication, no indication by the doctors that anything was wrong. Yet moments after Yanara had been born, Nila had fallen into a deep sleep, one that they had been unable to wake her from. She had remained that way for several days, before finally slipping away in the night.

Yanara had never known her mother. Moras had been younger, so he hadn't processed the deeper meaning of it. But Tonas had. Tonas had responded with sadness, then anger, and finally a cold acceptance. Perhaps it was because of this that Osran noticed he had always maintained a distance from Yanara. She didn't notice it yet, but if it continued then it would certainly have an impact as she grew older.

It wasn't her fault, but her birth had shaken the family to its core.

"Father?" Yanara's curious tone brought his attention back to the present. "Why are you sad?"

Osran smiled at her. He was known for tempering his emotions, but he always struggled when he thought of Nila. "Oh, it's nothing little one."

Yanara looked at him and narrowed her eyes, as though trying to figure something out. Suddenly her eyes widened and she threw her arms around his neck. "I know you miss Mother. I know you think of her when you look at me. I'm sorry."

Osran froze, the colour draining from his face. Ciloni gasped and clapped her free hand to her mouth.

"My lord, is she…?" Ciloni began to ask with a concerned look on her face.

But Osran didn't hear her. Yanara's words echoed in his mind, over and over like he was stuck in a loop. How could she know what he had been thinking? He'd never spoken to her of such things, or to anyone else. He kept his feelings buried, lest they consume him. So how did she know?

The feeling began to leave his fingers, a cold numbness creeping up his hands. He lowered Yanara to the ground as a suspicion grew in his mind, followed by a sinking realization.

"Ciloni," he said, his voice trembling. "Please take my son inside. You are not to speak of this to him, Tonas or anyone else. Do you understand?"

"But my lord—" Ciloni started, before a sharp look from Osran cut her off.

"Not a word to anyone. Inside, now."

Ciloni beckoned to Moras and then ushered him inside, who

glanced back at his father in grave concern before disappearing into the keep. A few moments later Osran was alone in the courtyard with his daughter.

"Yanara, come and sit with me," he said, leading her to a stone bench. She was quiet now, painfully aware that she had said something wrong.

"Father? What did I do? I'm sorry."

"Hush, child. I want you to tell me how you know what I was thinking. Can you do that for me?"

She looked at her feet, refusing to answer.

"Yanara, I'm not angry. But it's important you tell me."

Raising her head to look at him, she gulped before answering. "I-I don't really know, Father. When I looked at you, I felt you being sad. And I saw Mother in your head. I've seen her in there before, when you were sad other times."

Osran's heart sank. His girl, his beautiful little girl, could do something most others couldn't even understand. She could see into people's hearts and minds. She could read them like open books, and that made her dangerous.

She had the power of Mun, and people would kill her for it.

* * *

YANARA'S SCREAMS ECHOED through the chamber as Osran fought back tears, his chin trembling at the sound of his daughter's anguish. He rounded on the robed man stood next to him, fists clenched in anger.

"You told me she wouldn't feel any pain!" he said through gritted teeth.

"Forgive me, my lord," the man said in a soft voice. "I believe I said she *may* not feel any pain. We rarely conduct this procedure on one so young. Their minds are less…complicated, so there should have been less strain." He considered her for a moment, his forehead creasing as he frowned slightly. "Indeed, she appears to be suffering less than the others. However, I cannot say for certain what her experience is. Pain is so subjective."

Osran ground his teeth and turned back to the plinth that Yanara lay on. Heavy leather straps held her arms and legs in place, and her little head was completely enveloped in a hood of glowing crystal.

Other robed men stood around her, their hands stretched out as they chanted in an unknown language. Purple smoke flowed from their hands and into the strange crystal, which pulsed in time with Yanara's screams. Her little fingernails clawed at the stone, and her toes curled and uncurled in relentless agony.

What have I done to you, my darling girl?

After realising what Yanara was, Osran had ordered a carriage prepared and left Kyir that night. No driver, no aides. Just the two of them on the road to Selossa, the capital of Selathar. He'd kept her asleep with moon oil for the entire journey, mainly so she wouldn't panic, but also because he couldn't bear the thought of having to spend several days lying to her about why they were going there.

Deep under the capital were the Vaults of the Paragon, where the few Selathi practitioners of Mun worked to prepare the future rulers of their nation. Known to the Houselords as the Vault Masters, these strange mystics spent their entire lives underground. Children born with these powers, known as Mun savants, were taken from their families at birth. Once they entered the Vaults they would never see daylight again.

Osran was a man of considerable influence, however, and had managed to convince the Vault Masters to allow him to keep him daughter. There was a price, though, as with all deals.

"Tell me again about the seal," Osran asked. "How do we keep her safe?"

The master looked at him, studying him with cold eyes. "It will not be easy, my lord. The seal is strong, but only as strong as her heart. If her heart breaks, so does the seal. If so, her memories will return and her powers with them. The same will happen if she is ever told what she is. I cannot stress enough how important it is that she remains balanced and ignorant of the truth. And...there is one other thing."

"What is it?" Osran asked, frowning. If what the man had just said was true, he couldn't risk Yanara falling in love and having her heart broken. What else would he have to contend with?

"This will affect you as much as her, my lord. Your inevitable change in behaviour has the potential to cause her great emotional distress. From experience, I can tell you there are two choices for you."

"Such as?"

"You can learn to repress your feelings about these events, and quickly."

That would be difficult. The realisation that his daughter was a Mun savant had shattered Osran's reality, throwing everything he believed about his family into chaos.

"And the other choice?" he asked, hoping it would be at least somewhat less painful.

"If you cannot pretend, and you cannot control your emotions, you must find somewhere else for the blame to be placed. If you know in your heart that you will always harbour hurtful feelings for your daughter, you must convince her that it is for a reason entirely other than the fact she is a Mun savant. Otherwise, she will begin to question herself. And that is the beginning of a tragic ending for all concerned, I promise you."

"You want me to lie?"

"Yes! You must, my lord! Otherwise all this will have been for naught. Think hard of something you can use."

How could he think of a reason to hate his daughter? She had been everything to him. Such a beautiful child, full of life and—

His breath caught in his throat as he found himself running through the same thoughts again. She reminded him of Nila. Every day, she reminded him of his dead wife.

Could that be it? Could he use his grief for Nila to keep his daughter under control?

Did he have a choice?

Yanara stopped screaming, and the masters withdrew from the chamber. She was still now, and Osran walked over to her. He ran a finger down the side of her face, which was soaked with cold sweat. This poor little girl was now a greater threat to the fabric of their family than anything else. The others would never understand, and Ciloni and Moras would have to be sworn to secrecy. So much to be done, all because she was a Mun savant. Osran allowed himself a moment of selfish anger, dipping his toe into a reservoir of emotion that he knew would be tapped every day for the rest of his life.

Once again, everything had changed. Because of her.

Because of Yanara.

CHAPTER THREE

THE CURIOUS SNAIL edged its way onto the gravel path, its tentacles searching ahead of it for food and potential predators. It had travelled an impressive distance across relatively exposed ground, escaping the gaze of the birds that nested in the courtyard trees of Vasso Keep. Safety was close, underneath the decking on the other side of the path, where the snail would find shade and moisture.

Alas, it was not to be.

Corin's foot landed on the unsuspecting snail with a crunch, followed by a soft squelch. He immediately yelped and hopped away, wiping his shoe on the grass with a disgusted face. Giving a visible shudder, he turned around and waved frantically.

"Chessa, I just stood on a snail! It's horrible!"

"Says the snail killer," his twin sister Vishki retorted from her perch atop the fountain, a wry smile creeping onto her face.

Chuckling to herself, Chessa rose from the bench she had been perched on at the edge of the courtyard. She was a tall woman, standing a little over six feet in height with a strong, lithe frame. Her long, burgundy hair was pulled back into a braided ponytail, which presently trailed down over her shoulder and rested on the breast of her brown leather jerkin. A dark green hunting cloak was draped over her shoulders and hung down to her weathered thigh boots.

Into these boots were tucked her grey breeches, along with three small throwing daggers.

Chessa was the Companion Hunter, the most senior bodyguard to Houselord Vasso and his family. Holding this honoured position for eleven of the sixteen years she had been in service to Osran Vasso, Chessa executed her duties with utmost loyalty and care. She accompanied her Lord whenever he left Kyir and was responsible for the security of the noble House.

Studying Corin and his sister Vishki with discerning blue eyes, she considered how the dynamic of her service had changed since the twins had been born. Previously, she had spent most of her time with Lord Vasso and his son Tonas, joining their hunts and protecting them from those who would see harm come to them. As the children had been born, Tonas had requested that she watch over them and ensure they remained safe.

Chessa had never liked children. She considered them to be annoying and unpredictable, with a tendency to cause trouble at the most inopportune moments. As she had watched the twins grow and mature, however, she had found herself growing very attached to them. To her horror, as their third birthday passed, she 34ecogniz that she loved them as though they were her own children.

"You're both idiots," came a voice from behind her.

Chessa rolled her eyes and turned to look at Sima, Yanara's daughter. She had been sat at the other end of the courtyard, reading a book and pretending not to be interested.

She was nothing like the twins. Whereas they were warm, playful and a pleasure to be around, Sima was cold, spoilt and thoroughly disagreeable. She refused to respond to anyone but her mother, who had convinced her that she was nothing short of the next heir to the seat of House Vasso.

That, of course, was impossible, Chessa thought. Sima was a half Selathi, half Akhani bastard, born out of wedlock and raised by her mother. Her pale skin and black hair gave her away as having the strong blood of the Akhanu, which meant she would never have fit in even if she hadn't been a contemptuous little troll.

"Sima, mind your tongue," Chessa chided. "You shouldn't speak to heirs in such a manner, even if your mother does."

The girl made a disgusted noise in the back of her throat, and returned to her reading.

Vishki was walking over to her brother, and Chessa crossed the courtyard to join them. Looking up at her, Corin awkwardly attempted to present the sole of his shoe for inspection. Losing his balance, he promptly fell into the nyberry bush behind him. In a rare display of outward emotion, Vishki collapsed into a fit of giggles, causing a smile to creep onto Chessa's face again. She reached out and grasped the boy's arm, pulling him to his feet and surveying him.

"You've managed to stain your new shirt, Master Corin. I doubt Steward Juhan will be pleased."

Corin snorted. "Juhan is never pleased. He's been mean and nasty since his wife died."

"That's an awful thing to say!" Vishki admonished. "Madam Noya was lovely, and you liked her too."

"I did, but Juhan is still a grumpy old man."

Shaking her head, Chessa gave him a disapproving stare. "Such offhand remarks will not serve you well in your later years, young Master. You can't go through life saying the first thing that comes into your head." A lesson that some of the Household staff would do well to learn, especially the maids. They tended to gossip without checking who was nearby.

Corin opened his mouth to respond but was distracted by movement from the far side of the courtyard. Turning to see who was approaching, Chessa instantly recognized the twins' father.

Deran Vasso was a handsome man, with the characteristic brown hair and hazel eyes of the Vasso family. A keen hunter with an athletic build, he was a little taller than Chessa, though the thick soles of her boots tended to make up the difference. Though popular with the ladies of Kyir, he remained a respectful distance from women ever since the death of his wife. Giva had died young, an unfortunate victim of the Lharasan phage which ravaged Kyir two years previously. The disease had been carried by a trader, and it had killed a good third of the town's population before the doctors had managed to isolate and eliminate it.

Deran had grieved deeply for a full year, and even now he was still not himself. A sadness filled his eyes, and though he often smiled, those around him could see his heart was empty. Chessa longed to see him return to be the cheerful, lively father that the twins deserved.

She also longed for something more, something that she knew could never happen. Forcing a smile onto her face as he drew near, she offered a bow. Vishki ran over to hug her father, and he embraced her awkwardly, as though it caused him pain.

"Little one, your hugs are getting too strong!"

"Don't be silly, Father!" Vishki chuckled, then released him. "I could never hurt you!"

Corin appeared at his father's side, looking up at Deran with a toothy grin.

"Father, I stood on a snail. Am I in trouble?"

"Did you do it on purpose?"

"…no."

"Then you're fine by me. Just make sure the snail's family don't find you."

A panicked look crept onto Corin's face as his eyes started scanning the floor for vengeful molluscs. Deran and Vishki laughed, and Chessa chuckled again.

"Be nice, my lord. Your son has a vivid imagination—we wouldn't want him fretting over nothing."

Deran laughed again as his son gave him a solid kick in the shin, then stomped away to sit on a stone step and sulk. He turned to Chessa, his expression becoming soft.

"How are you, Chessa?" he asked, with a warm smile on his face.

Her heart pounded in her chest, and she looked away as she felt her face flush.

"I—I am well, my lord. It's been a quiet morning, though the twins have kept me busy for most of it. I would have preferred to be with your father, but he insisted that only family were to be present."

"Don't feel so bad," Deran said, giving her a smile that left her short of breath. "Father wouldn't allow me to be there either. Too much fuss always made my grandfather uncomfortable."

"Do you think it's happened? Do you think he's passed on?"

"I think we're about to find out," Deran replied, nodding towards the end of the courtyard where Sima sat. As Chessa turned to see Yanara stalking across the grass towards them, Sima closed her book and fell in step beside her, adopting her usual air of superiority that she held whenever her mother was around.

"My lady," Chessa said, offering her the slightest bow. Deran said nothing, which didn't surprise her. He was an outspoken critic of his aunt and the way she battled with his father.

"Chessa, leave. I have business with my nephew."

"I serve at Lord Deran's request, my lady. Not yours."

"You should take care when you speak to me, hunter," Yanara said with a threatening tone, her hand closing around the handle of her rapier. "Your old lord isn't around to protect you now."

Chessa struggled to maintain her composure, but it was Deran who spoke.

"What are you saying, aunt?"

Yanara adopted an expression of mock grief. "Our Lord Osran has passed."

Chessa felt a stab of pain in her heart. Lord Osran had been like a father to her since she was young. Her loyalty to him was second to none, and in many ways he had been the focal point of her existence before the twins arrived. She fought back tears and steeled her nerve.

"And my father? He is named?" Deran asked, his voice trembling.

"He is," Yanara said with a scowl. "*Long may he live.*"

Deran looked at his children. "This could not have come at a worse time," he said quietly, continuing to watch them. "The twins will need you, Chessa, now more than ever."

"I understand, my Lord," she replied with a gentle nod. "I will continue to watch over them, but I must swear my oath soon. My duty is to Houselord Vasso, no matter who it is."

"Chessa, he's surrounded by your fellow Hunters. Your oath can wait. For now, I need you here whilst I tell the children."

She bowed her head in deference to Deran. Her oath was to the House as well as its Lord, and the heirs had the authority of their fathers. She beckoned the children over, who had been fussing over a cat hiding under the bushes. They made one last feeble attempt to draw it out, then stood up and walked over to their father. Deran took a knee and placed a hand on each of their shoulders.

"Do you two remember what I told you about being heirs? About your responsibility?"

Vishki nodded. "You said that we would have to grow up quickly, and that we couldn't stay children forever."

"What's happened, Father?" Corin asked.

Deran sighed, and stood up. "Your great grandfather Osran has passed away."

The twins stood in silence for a moment, trying to process the news. Corin started crying, whilst Vishki said nothing.

"Your grandfather Tonas is the new Houselord, which makes me the new heir."

Vishki frowned, as though trying to work something out in her head. Chessa saw Deran raise an eyebrow and meet her gaze. "What is it, Vish?" he asked.

"What about great aunt Yanara? She was born after Grampy Osran but before you. Isn't she next in line?"

"Because," Yanara interjected, "you will find that life is unfair that way. Especially when you are a woman. Perhaps your father will be kind enough to teach you how the world works someday. Or maybe someone else will teach you sooner."

She locked eyes with Deran, and for a moment Chessa thought they were about to have an argument. But Yanara's expression softened almost immediately, and she held out her hand to her daughter. "Come Sima."

The two of them retreated into the keep, leaving Deran and Chessa alone with the twins.

"We've been through this, Vishki," Deran continued. "That's not how the line of succession works. It runs down through each firstborn child, and unfortunately your aunt was the thirdborn after Uncle Moras."

Corin was still crying. Vishki frowned again. "But what about Uncle Kalim? He was firstborn to Grampy."

"Vishki, this isn't the time," Deran replied. "Someday soon I will explain it to you again."

Vishki's expression softened. "Oh, okay." She turned and wandered over to Chessa and Corin and wrapped her arms around them both.

Chessa considered how strange Vishki was in terms of her emotional reactions. She wasn't an overtly outgoing child, but she clearly understood the emotions of others. Something she got from her father and grandfather, apparently, which reminded Chessa of the pending negotiations. She looked up at Deran. "What of the negotiations, my lord? Will they still go ahead?"

Deran scratched his chin. "I expect they will. Father said that

Lord Osran was adamant that we don't postpone them, or we risk offending our guests."

"When do we expect their arrival?"

As if to answer her, a horn sounded three short blasts outside the grounds of the Keep.

House Talet was here.

CHAPTER FOUR

Twenty-one years ago

"YANARA! PAY ATTENTION!"

The sound of her governess' harsh voice echoing through her eardrums made Yanara drop her needle, which hit the floor and rolled under the wooden bureau she was sat next to. Her attention had been drawn to the corner of a bookshelf where an epic battle was being fought between a spider and a woodfly that had become entangled in its web. The woodfly's desperate struggle for freedom was fascinating to her although she also considered that a web being there in the first place meant the servants were not doing their cleaning duties properly.

Letting out a frustrated sigh, she slid off her chair and laid on her stomach, scrabbling about for the pencil in the dust underneath the bureau.

"And get off the floor in your dress! Young ladies should not be rolling around in the dust and dirt."

Her governess, Katyana, was a strict woman who spent many hours a day drilling lessons into Yanara. The proper sensibilities of women, she would say, were not to be ignored. As the only daughter of Osran Vasso, it was expected that she conduct herself impeccably, as many eyes would be on her as she grew up.

Not that Yanara particularly cared for such things, much to Katyana's chagrin. She was far more interested in the sort of activities her brothers got up to, like hunting, fighting, and learning how to lead a House. As the thirdborn and youngest child, as well as being a girl, she would never have to worry about being responsible for representing House Vasso in diplomacy or negotiations. That didn't stop her from taking an interest, however, no matter how many times her father and governess tried to push her towards more ladylike pursuits.

"Up, up!" Katyana's voice rattled through her head again.

Rolling her eyes, Yanara clambered to her feet and brushed the dust off her dress, which was stitched from a beautiful aquamarine velvet. Her father had presented it to her as a gift after he had returned from his last trade visit to Akhatar, and there were few days she did not wear it. Gifts from Father were rare, meaning she appreciated them more than perhaps she otherwise would have.

Adjusting her hair, she laced her fingers together in front of her as she had been taught and gave Katyana a steely look.

"Better, ma'am?" she said tartly.

Katyana gave her a disapproving stare, then clicked her fingers at one of the attendant maids, who hurriedly retrieved the needle from under the bureau. Dusting it off with her apron, she placed it carefully next to the sewing Yanara had casually dumped on the table. "As a lady, you must learn to let the servants do such things for you. It will not do to have you carrying out such mundane tasks, lest the line blurs between yourself and the common folk. Do you understand?"

"Yes," Yanara replied. "But I was only trying to be helpful."

"You can help by paying attention to your embroidery, and giving me some semblance of reassurance that you are making progress with your lessons. Your brothers have no issue sitting down and getting on with their studies. Perhaps you could learn a thing or two from them."

Yanara scowled at her. Whilst she was more drawn to their studies than her own, she was forbidden to undertake such pursuits. Even so, she was continually compared to her brothers in almost every aspect, which was beginning to grate on her. They were far older than she was, in their twenties, whilst she was only approaching her thirteenth birthday.

No matter how hard she tried to please Katyana and her father, nothing ever seemed to be enough. It left her feeling constantly tired, and more and more she wished she could be free to follow her own heart. The family didn't need her, and in many ways she felt they didn't even want her. She wondered whether things would have been different if Mother had still been alive.

Her heart wrenched at the thought of a mother she had never known. Nila had died giving birth to Yanara, something she felt her father and brothers had always held against her, though they would never admit to it. Having never known her mother, all she had to go on were the stories that Osran and Katyana would tell her.

By all accounts, Nila had been an impressive woman. Intelligent, confident, and beautiful beyond the dreams of most women, the stories Yanara had heard said that Nila refused his proposal three times before she finally said yes, and had accompanied him back to Kyir to take her place at his side as the matriarch of House Vasso.

Yanara wished she had known her mother. If nothing else, she hoped in her heart that Nila would have given her the attention her father never had.

She'd managed so far, however, and as she grew older she was becoming more aware that dreaming for the impossible wouldn't change anything.

"Ma'am, why am I learning all this?" she asked, folding her arms across her chest.

"I would have thought that would be obvious. It is expected that a lady be prepared to undertake such activities."

"But why? If I'm such a noble lady, as you keep telling me, won't I have servants to do all this for me? Sewing is hardly something I imagine Mother used to do."

She winced as Katyana slapped the table with her hand. "Your mother was an extraordinary woman, and did more for this House than you will ever know, young lady. She knew her responsibilities, and she didn't shy away from hard work for one moment. You are a stark contrast from the woman she was, Eratia rest her soul."

The final words broke Yanara's stubborn spirit, and she burst into tears, burying her head in her hands. She wanted so much to believe that Mother would have been proud of her, but Katyana was right. How could she be like her mother, when all she had were stories of her?

She felt arms around her, and she buried her face into Katyana's dress, letting the tears flow.

"I'm sorry, young one," said the governess. Her voice was softer than Yanara had ever heard it. "I allowed my emotions to get the better of me, and I should have controlled my tongue. It appears you are not the only one who still has things to learn."

* * *

LATER THAT NIGHT, as Yanara sat at dinner with the family, she plucked up the courage to ask a question that she had never dared to pose. Tonas and Ciloni were sat down one side of the table with Kalim and Deran between them, occasionally breaking up the small scuffles they got into when they thought nobody was looking.

She was sat on the opposite side next to Moras, talking about her lessons.

"Um, Father?" she asked, nervously playing with the vegetables on her plate. "Do you hate me?"

Looking at her with a bemused expression on his face, Osran chuckled. "Of course not, my daughter. Why do you ask?"

"Well," Yanara said, taking a deep breath, "I feel like you all hate me because of Mother. Like it's my fault she's dead."

Osran looked at her in stunned silence, a chunk of meat falling off the fork suspended over his plate. Tonas and Moras looked at each other nervously, waiting for an explosion of anger from their father. Whilst not a generally angry man, his temper could be terrible when he was upset.

There was an unspoken agreement amongst the family that they didn't speak of Nila or her death. Tonas had made an offhand comment in his teenage years which had resulted in a harsh beating, and since then he had been harder on Moras and Yanara about their mother than anyone.

On this occasion, however, Osran showed no sign of anger. He simply laid down his cutlery, wiped his mouth with his napkin, and sat back in his chair. "All of you, leave us," he said in a quiet voice.

"But Father, we haven't finished our food," Moras complained.

Osran shot him a dangerous look, causing him to cower in his seat. Moras was smaller than his brother, as well as being six years his junior. He hadn't inherited the same sense of confidence and reckless bravado that Tonas had demonstrated in his youth, instead proving himself to be a gentle and considerate young man.

"We'll take it into the drawing room," Tonas said quickly. He nodded at his brother and gestured to Ciloni and the boys. "Come on!"

The five of them grabbed their plates and headed out of the dining room. As they left, Moras gave Yanara an awkward smile. Out of her two brothers, she had always gotten on better with Moras. They both knew what it felt like to live in Tonas' shadow as the heir, and Moras had a soft side that she empathised with. He often stole her away from Katyana's gaze to teach her things like archery and politics, and the two of them had developed a close bond. A bond she wished she shared with her father and eldest brother.

"Yanara, come here." Osran's voice brought her attention back to earth.

Rising from her chair, she walked around the table to where her father sat. Taking her hands in his, he looked at her with sad eyes.

"Why would you ask such a thing?" Osran gripped her hands slightly.

"You never pay any attention to me," she said, looking at the floor. "You always focus on Tonas and Moras, but I'm here too. I feel like you and Tonas blame me for Mother's death, and although Moras doesn't say anything I know he sometimes feels the same way."

Osran placed a hand on her cheek. "Look at me, Yanara," he said softly. She raised her head to meet his gaze. "You are my daughter, and a member of House Vasso. I do not hate you, nor do I blame you for your mother's death."

She smiled weakly at the words, feeling some sense of relief.

"However," Osran continued, "you are here on this earth, and she is not. Whatever gods sit in the Heavens playing their games saw fit to take her from me, like a cruel joke. And every time I look at your face I am reminded of that the fact that she is gone. Whenever I see your eyes, your hair, the way you talk and move, I see her in you. And it kills me, Yanara. It kills me that I am so close to her, to who she was, yet I can never have her in my life again. So you see, whilst it is not your fault, your very existence causes me pain. And that is something that will never change whilst you are in this House."

It was as though he had plunged an ice cold stake into her heart.

She stared as him, her mouth open in disbelief. This wasn't what she had expected at all. Not once in her moments of self reflection and wondering had she imagined such words coming from his mouth.

Wrenching her hands out of his grip, Yanara stepped away and stumbled backwards. In that moment, she saw him for who he truly was. A man twisted by his grief and position into a cold, unfeeling monster. Until those words had left his lips, she had kept some hope in her heart that they could someday love one another as father and daughter.

That day would never come.

Tears welling up in her eyes, she turned and fled from the room. As she approached the door, she heard him speak, his voice strong and cold again.

"Oh, and Yanara? Please send the rest of the family back in on your way out," Osran said, lifting his fork to his mouth. "At least they know how to make civil conversation over dinner."

She ran to her room, not bothering to knock for Tonas and Moras.

CHAPTER FIVE

A PECULIAR FEELING gripped Tonas as he awoke that morning to the sun shining through his window, one that sat in the back of his mind like an unwelcome house guest. He couldn't quite put his finger on it, but it left him uneasy as he allowed his attendants to bathe and dress him. He dismissed it as simple nerves and reminded himself that he had an important day ahead. After all, entering into negotiations on your first day as Houselord would be enough to leave anyone on edge.

As the attendants finished their routine, there came a knock on the door.

"Enter," Tonas said loudly. He wondered if he was overdoing the authoritative voice, but then again it was unlikely anyone would correct him if he was.

Juhan, the House Steward, entered the room with a gentle smile. A kindly man in his twilight years, he'd served their family for over forty years, and still had the same twinkle in his eye that Tonas remembered from his childhood.

"My lord, Lady Ciloni begs you join her at the breakfast table. She seems intent on ensuring you eat a full and proper meal before you start your day, and I must say I agree with her," Juhan said with a chuckle. "Good food and a stout drink are sufficient to prepare any man for the rigours of daily lordship."

Tonas smiled at him. He had a way of soothing nerves and calming the fiercest rage. Even Father's temper had been doused by a few well-chosen words from Juhan on occasion. "Please tell my lady that I will be with her shortly. And perhaps give her a cup of wine to ease her worrying mind."

"As you say, my Lord," Juhan replied with a bow, before disappearing out of the room.

Good stewards were rare in the outer provinces of Selathar. Most of them flocked to the capital and the more cultured towns, where employment was easier to come by. Juhan was getting older, and soon the day would come where Tonas would be faced with the prospect of having to find a replacement, and that was a task he did not look forward to.

Adjusting his new clothes, Tonas stood in front of the mirror and considered the man who looked back at him. Yesterday he had awoken as Tonas, son of Osran. Today, he was Houselord Vasso. That would take some getting used to.

He took a deep breath and turned from the mirror, opening the adjoining door that led into the family dining room where Ciloni was waiting for him.

"It's about time, husband of mine," she said with a wry smile. "I was starting to think the attendants had done away with you."

Planting a kiss on her forehead, he smiled at her. "I'm sorry to have kept you, my love. I might be Houselord to everyone else, but without you I am just a man."

Ciloni rolled her eyes as she tore a piece off the bread on her plate and popped it into his mouth. "Stop talking and eat, dear. You need your strength if you're going to deal with that Talet boy today."

Tonas frowned as he chewed the fresh bread, considering what he knew of the son of Imdan Talet. Naidar had a reputation as something of a fool, but he didn't put much stock in common gossip. He preferred to form his own opinion of people, which had often frustrated those who liked nothing better than to berate others in an attempt to curry favour.

It begged an interesting question, though. If Imdan was keen on these negotiations, why hadn't he come himself? It was true that as his firstborn son, Naidar should be given the opportunity to represent his father and prepare himself for his own lordship, but all the reports from Manar suggested that Imdan despised his son.

Perhaps the Houselord had found some mote of confidence in his son and decided to give him a chance, but Tonas had no way of knowing. All he could do was enter these negotiations with a calm and determined head and pray that the boy would do the same.

"You're overthinking things again, Tonas."

Ciloni's words brought him back to reality, and he swallowed the bread before offering her a nervous smile. "Not for the last time, I suspect. Do you think these negotiations will yield anything?"

"Even if they don't, you cannot pass up the opportunity to make new friends. The alliances between Houses are what keeps our nation together, as well as our families."

She was of course referring to their marriage. Ciloni was a daughter of House Nura, the ruling family of Parello, a port town to the east. In the latter days of the Last Province War, Lharasan raiders had swept down the coast of Western Selathar putting Evellim and Manar to the torch, and would have done the same to Kyir had it not been for timely reinforcements from Parello. House Nura had seen fit to come to their aid, and together their forces had pushed back the barbarians beyond the northern mountains that separated Selathar and Lharasar.

In recognition of this act and in eternal gratitude, Hannis Vasso, the Houselord at the time, had sworn that each heir would marry a daughter of House Nura so long as there was one of appropriate age. Osran had not been matched to a Nura daughter when he met Nila, which Tonas knew he was grateful for. Asking him to give up Nila would have been almost impossible.

So it was that Tonas became betrothed to Ciloni at a young age, in honour of the agreement made between their two Houses. Originally uncomfortable with the idea, he had warmed to it once he had met her. She was an average looking girl, but fiercely intelligent and exceptionally witty. Tonas found himself falling in love with her ability to hold her own in conversation, and their marriage had certainly not been dull.

His thoughts were interrupted by the door to the dining room flying open as Deran's twins raced in, giggling and jostling to get to the table first. Deran himself was not far behind and appeared visibly embarrassed by the ruckus they were causing.

"I apologise, Father," he said sheepishly. "They were so excited to see you on your first morning as Houselord."

"As they rightly should be, for the new Houselord Vasso." Chessa had entered the room, and as Tonas turned to her she dropped to a knee and bowed her head in respect. "My lord, I serve at your command."

"Chessa, please stand. I told you last night I didn't want these displays of fealty every time you see me."

Looking embarrassed, Chessa stood and nodded slightly. "As you say, my lord."

"And as for you two," Tonas said sternly as he placed his hands on his hips and fixed his gaze on the twins, "how dare you rush in here and not give your grandfather a hug?"

Corin rushed over to Tonas and wrapped his arms around the Houselord's waist, whilst Vishki rolled her eyes and walked calmly over to wait her turn. As Corin released him and Vishki offered him one of her rare embraces, he considered how different they were. Corin was emotional, Vishki much less so. In many ways they reminded him of his own siblings, a thought which caused him pain. He had never been particularly close to his brother or sister, and he felt the absence of their love so strongly now. Moras had been dead for three years, and Yanara might as well be for all the affection she felt for him.

He shook his head and patted Vishki's head as he extracted himself from her arms. "I have to be going, little one. Much to do before I sit down with our guests this morning. Chessa, I am entrusting you to greet Naidar Talet on my behalf."

Startled, Chessa paused for a moment as she struggled to find the words to respond. "My lord, that is an honour reserved for someone of more importance than I."

"You are the Companion Hunter, Chessa. Besides my blood, there is nobody more important. You will take Steward Juhan and introduce yourself, before escorting Naidar and his advisor to the Great Hall. I must speak with my sister."

He saw Chessa's eyes narrow at the mention of Yanara. Whilst respectful of all members of his family, Chessa had made no secret of the fact that she despised his sister. Her oath to Osran had made her fiercely protective of him, and Yanara's openly ill-mannered attitude towards the old man had almost brought them to blows on several occasions.

It was Tonas' hope that Chessa would feel less of a personal attachment to him, and in doing so she might relent in her internal persecution of Yanara. He could certainly do without the tension in the years to come.

"As it pleases you, my lord," Chessa responded. "Though I would rather not leave you alone with those who have…questionable motives."

"Chessa, that is quite enough," Tonas chided. "Your concern is reassuring, but I will not have it straying into outright accusations. Do I make myself clear?"

"Oh, I believe you do brother." Yanara was stood in the doorway with her arms folded, watching the conversation unfold with great amusement. "Look at her, she can barely contain her frustration," she said in a smug tone that made Tonas grit his teeth.

Deciding it would be better to remove her from the situation before Chessa put a knife through her heart, Tonas bowed to his family and strode from the room. "Yanara, with me. Now," he said in a commanding voice. She tutted before turning to follow him, and Tonas was sure he could hear Chessa's teeth grinding in the dining room. "Sister, I trust this morning finds you well."

"Of course it does," replied Yanara. "Watching you take that Lharasan bitch down a notch certainly makes my day just that little bit brighter."

"Watch your tongue, Yanara. She is still the Companion Hunter and she is still sworn to me. You're lucky you're my sister, otherwise I'm not sure even I could stop her from sticking a blade in you."

"She's welcome to try. But you didn't drag me out of the way just to save little old me, did you? You want to know about the Talet heir, and it's about time. I've spent many years trying to organise these negotiations, and despite resistance from you and Osran we are finally allowing the Talets into our halls."

"I still have my reservations, Yanara. Had it not been Father's last wish I would have postponed these negotiations, perhaps even cancelled them."

Yanara narrowed her eyes at Tonas and folded her arms across her chest. "You would disrespect his will? He saw the value of these negotiations in the end, even if you still don't. I had hoped you had learned from his legacy, but perhaps I was wrong. We'll just have to see if you can handle the pressures of being Houselord."

Tonas straightened up and fixed Yanara with an icy glare,

causing her to take a step back. "I will not have you question me, Yanara. I will conduct these talks in good faith, and with the best interests of House Vasso in mind. You will play your part accordingly in there, and if you do anything to harm the negotiations you will have shown where your true loyalties lie."

"Of course...*my lord*," Yanara replied softly. "I remain, as always, loyal to our House."

His stance softening, Tonas motioned for Yanara to walk with him. "I know we didn't have an easy childhood, Yanara. I know I wasn't the brother I should have been, but I had so many expectations placed on me. We've both made mistakes, but perhaps mine were the gravest."

He stopped as Yanara placed a hand on his shoulder, the first time she'd touched him in years. A sudden feeling of calm washed over him. "That's not important now, brother. We have other matters to attend to, matters far more current than any transgressions either of us have made in the past."

He smiled at her, though she did not return it. Perhaps that had been too much to expect from her. Instead he turned and carried on down the hallway, Yanara always half a step behind him.

"Tell me what to expect, Yanara. I've heard the rumours, of course, but you've met the man himself. Tell me about Naidar Talet."

* * *

CHESSA CLENCHED HER jaw as she knocked on the door of the guest chamber for the third time, causing the hinges to rattle.

"Perhaps he is asleep, Lady Hunter?" Juhan suggested as he shrugged his shoulders at her.

They had been supposed to meet Naidar half an hour ago, but when he hadn't arrived on time they had gone looking for him. His advisor was nowhere to be seen either, which was more disconcerting.

"This is ridiculous," Chessa grumbled. "A man should not be late to negotiations, especially not as the guest of a Houselord. And where is the other one? The advisor?"

She clicked her fingers at one of the guards stood nearby, who snapped sharply to attention and marched over.

"Yes, ma'am?" he asked.

"Have either of our *distinguished* guests left their chambers this morning, Nybek?"

"Not that I've seen, ma'am. When I relieved Omoris earlier this morning, he did note that there'd been neither sight nor sound of them all night either."

Chessa stared at him. "So you're telling me that we have the heir to House Talet and his advisor wandering somewhere around the keep?"

"Well, not wandering ma'am. They should be in their chambers?"

"Should be? How do you know if you haven't checked on them?"

"Well, it's not right to be disturbing an heir in his private chambers, ma'am. Disrespectful and all."

She sighed, and massaged her temples. "What on earth do I train you men for? Go and check on his advisor, now. Force the door open if you have to."

Nybek turned and disappeared down the hallway towards the other guest chambers.

Juhan chuckled. "You're too harsh on them, Lady Hunter. They're just trying to do their jobs without upsetting anyone."

"They're soldiers, Juhan, not stewards. Their job is to ensure that everyone in this keep is safe, which they can't do if they don't know their whereabouts."

"True, but you might go a little easier on them. I remember you being much the same when you first came to us."

She sighed and looked Juhan in the eye. He was right of course, as he often was. As a younger member of the Keep's retinue, she had often made mistakes that warranted…corrective instruction. Juhan himself had taught her much about how to behave around lords and ladies, which had equipped her with the knowledge necessary to hold her own against the politics of court.

"My lord, please!" Nybek was shouting down the corridor, which caught Chessa's attention. A man she took to be Naidar's advisor was strolling down the corridor with an angry expression on his face. As he approached them, he stopped and calmed himself with a deep breath.

"My lady Chessa, I presume?" he asked. "Houselord Tonas'

Companion Hunter?"

"At your service, my lord...?" She trailed off, realising she'd neglected to learn his name before greeting him.

"Javin will suffice. I understand you're having trouble rousing my Lord Naidar?"

"Yes, though we were concerned at your absence as well. Is everything all right?"

"Hmm?" Javin looked distracted. "Oh yes, all is well. If you'll excuse me." He hammered on the door even harder than Chessa had. "Naidar! Naidar, you are late! Open this door!" No sound came from within the room. Javin turned to them and gave an embarrassed smile. "I trust you have the key to this door?"

"Right here, my lord," Nybek replied, eager to appease Chessa after his apparent neglect.

"Then by all means, please open it."

Nybek looked at him nervously, then at Chessa for approval, She nodded at him and folded her arms across her chest, curious to see what Javin would do. He seemed not to hold the usual level of respect for his lord, and she was interested to see their relationship for herself.

Inserting the key into the lock, Nybek turned it and stepped back in shock as Javin slammed the door open and strode into the room. Hurrying in behind him, Chessa almost gasped at the sight that greeted her.

Judging by the smashed jug and red stains on the carpet, Naidar Talet had clearly decided that the best thing to do before an important negotiation was to consume as much wine as possible. Not only that, but he'd collapsed on the bed completely naked and defecated over himself before passing out.

If he hadn't been a guest and an heir to a noble House, Chessa might have considered it a solid effort on his part. Javin was not as impressed.

"NAIDAR!" he roared, kicking the young man awake. "What on earth do you call this!?"

Naidar looked around him as his eyes fluttered open, wiping dried vomit off his lips. "Ah, Javin. Be a good fellow and fetch me some clothes would you? And a wench? That one will do nicely," he said, gesturing at Chessa. She felt the colour rising in her cheeks as her fists began to clench uncontrollably. How dare this man abuse their hospitality and then insult her honour?

Clearly noticing her face was like thunder, Juhan placed a hand on her arm. "Lady Hunter, perhaps I should deal with this?" he said gently. "Please tell our Houselord that I will have Lord Naidar to him within the hour, washed, dressed and fed."

"Ah yes!" Naidar said, waving the handle of a broken wine cup at them. "Tell Tonas I look forward to meeting him."

Chessa opened her mouth to retort at his disrespectful use of her Houselord's first name but was silenced by a look from Juhan who pushed her out of the door and into the hallway.

"Go, Lady Hunter. See to our Lord if you please."

With that the door shut in her face, leaving her alone in the corridor save for Nybek who was busy sniggering.

"And what are you laughing at?" Chessa snapped at him. "Go ahead and make your jokes, but that man in there still shits more money that you'll ever have in your life. Think of that the next time you let a guest drink himself into such a dishonourable state."

She left Nybek to ponder on his morning's mistakes, quietly cursing herself for wanting to join in his ridicule.

CHAPTER SIX

Fourteen years ago

"GET OUT!"

The shoe hit the young man squarely in the face, causing him to stumble backwards and trip over the threshold of the door. He landed on his back in the hallway, cracking his head on the polished stonework and leaving a small amount of blood seeping into the cracks between the slabs.

As Yanara retrieved her shoe from the doorway, she stood over the terrified man, a vision of indignant fury. Scowling at him, she wielded the shoe like a knife, waving it in his face as she continued her tirade.

"You can run and tell my father," she hissed, "that the next time he sends me some miserable wretch of a lordling to *inform me* that I'll be marrying him, I'll be sending a servant to *inform him* that he can collect the body himself. Understand, little man?"

Despite his obvious concussion, the man nodded frantically before scrambling to his feet and disappearing down the hallway. Yanara heard a brief scuffle, followed by the sound of him apologising profusely to someone who chuckled, a sound which was instantly recognisable as belonging to Moras.

"You know, assaulting the thirdborn son of House Kivellen may not be the best way to court their favour," he said as he arrived at her door. She made a disgusted sound in her throat and strode back into the room as Moras tentatively followed her, almost like a frightened puppy.

"Thirdborn! THIRD! Osran doesn't even have the decency to send me an heir, or even a secondborn son," she exclaimed, brandishing the shoe as she wheeled around to face her brother. "I am not some kitchen mutt he can just feed scraps to in the hope I'll disappear."

Flinching at the footwear she was brandishing, Moras raised his hands to shield himself from a furious blow. "Sister, I really wish you would call him Father. It's not the done thing to refer to him by name in front of others."

"Why should I call him Father?" she demanded. "He barely considers me his daughter, and I won't pretend otherwise."

It had been seven years since that night in the dining room, and still Osran's words burned in her mind. For a few weeks afterwards, she had poured her heart and soul into trying to be a good daughter. She had tried to act, move and dress differently so she didn't remind him so much of her mother, but nothing changed. As the months and years went by, she stopped trying to gain his favour and began to assert her independence more and more. Part of her had hoped this would provoke a reaction from him, even an outburst.

But it was as though she didn't exist in his eyes. Of course he spoke to her, and acknowledged her when he had to, but she felt like a ghost to him. That just upset her more, and eventually she gave up caring. As long as he left her alone, she was content to walk the halls of Vasso Keep doing what she pleased.

That had all changed when she turned sixteen, and Osran had decided it was time for her to be married. The argument in the Great Hall between the two of them was the most emotional interaction they had ever had, and it lasted for half a day until Osran had Moras drag her back to her room.

For the next three years, various suitors had arrived in Kyir, hoping to win the hand of the sole daughter of the venerable Houselord Vasso. All of them had been rejected, and as time had gone on the quality of potential husbands had greatly diminished as more and more of them were put off by the stories of Yanara's foul temper. She was now nineteen, and though she despised the men who had come calling she had dreams of meeting a handsome rogue in a strange tavern, or something equally as fantastic.

"Besides," she said, "I'm surprised he even has time to think about such things considering how excessive his sense of self-importance is these days."

"It's not really self-importance if you're a Houselord," Moras said, rolling his eyes. "You can't get much more important in Selathar, Yanara. Unless you're the Paragon, but then again we'd be living in much grander surroundings if that were the case. Assuming of course that the Paragon would even be allowed to have children."

"Moras, I don't really care," she continued. "What I care about is being allowed to choose my own husband, instead of these…mealworms that come crawling into my chambers unannounced."

He grinned at her, closing the door so they wouldn't be interrupted.

"Why are you making that stupid face, idiot?" she asked, raising an eyebrow.

"Because I might have a way for you to do just that," he replied, his eyes lit up with mischievous intent.

"Stop scheming. You were never very good at it."

"Do you want my help or not?"

She sighed, sitting down on her bed. "Go on then, amaze me with your brilliant plan," she said, pretending to check under her fingernails.

"Father and Tonas are leaving in a week, and they're leaving me in charge!" The glee in his voice was so overpowering it almost made her wince. She stared at him with an incredulous look on her face.

"You? The soft-hearted jester of House Vasso?"

"Alright, there's no need to be a bitch about it. Father wanted Tonas to go with him on his next set of trade talks, and Tonas jumped at the chance of course. He talked Father into letting me head the House whilst they're gone, instead of the usual rabble of advisors."

"Good for you, brother. How does that help me?" Yanara maintained an unimpressed face.

"It helps you, because with Father and Tonas gone there's nobody left to keep you from going into town and meeting the man of your dreams." Moras grinned again, and this time she couldn't help but crack a smile.

"All right, you've got my attention. Will you also be sneaking off to visit some secret fling?" She poked him playfully in the chest.

"I'll have you know I'm making plans to meet my future husband before very long," he replied, looking longingly out of the window.

Yanara looked at him, puzzled. "Future husband? Have I met him?" she asked, wondering what she'd missed whilst she'd been exiling potential suitors.

"Oh, neither of us have. But I'm sure he'll be strong and handsome, like a blacksmith's apprentice or a dashing stable hand."

"Such lofty heights you reach for, brother," she teased, laughing as he pushed her back onto the bed. "Does Father know yet?"

"Of course he does, he just pretends he doesn't. You know what he's like, out of sight, out of mind." He stopped, looking sheepishly at Yanara. "Sorry," he said pulling an awkward face.

"Don't worry about it," she said. She'd long since given up caring about his unsubtle slip-ups. "So where are they going, anyway?"

"Oh, the usual places. Along the southern coast to Parello, then up to Tuam and The Citadel, and eventually into Akhatar."

Akhatar was an unknown world to her, a place she'd only read about in books. The militant Akhan, their strange complexions. All of it was fascinating to her, and she'd longed to escape the boredom of her life in Kyir for some time now.

If she could somehow convince Osran to take her with him, she would finally get to see more of the world. To understand what drove him to travel and meet new people. And of course, maybe she would get to meet someone new herself. Perhaps a dashing Akhani prince would sweep her off her feet and spirit her away to be wed.

It was worth a shot at least.

"Akhatar?" she asked, her interest piqued. "For how long?"

Moras looked at her, realisation dawning on him. "No, no. Don't even think about it Yanara, you know he won't allow it!" he said as she leapt off the bed and flung the door open.

"Then there's no harm in me asking is there?" she replied, giving him a mischievous grin before disappearing out the door and into the hallway.

As she strode towards her father's study, the setting sun casting golden light through the windows, she considered the request she was about to make. It was unlikely that Osran would grant her any request given the nature of their broken relationship, so she would have to give him something in return.

She begrudged giving him any such satisfaction, but it would only be temporary. The plan had formulated in her head so quickly she kept going over it for mistakes, but she could find none. Not unless you counted Osran saying no, but that was the only major obstacle, and she was convinced she could persuade him to agree to her proposal.

Arriving at the door to his study, she steeled herself in preparation for what she was about to do. The promise she was about to make was nothing compared to what would have to come first. She knocked on the door.

"Come," echoed the rough voice from the chamber beyond. She pushed the door open and stepped into the room.

Osran sat at his desk, busy writing letters in preparation for his journey with Tonas. He looked the same as ever, a tired old man with foolish dreams. She scowled briefly, then swallowed the lump in her throat.

"Father." Saying the word after so long made her nauseous. The man in front of her was no father to her, yet she had to be diplomatic if she was going to succeed in her little mission.

He looked up in surprise, studying her for a moment. Returning his quill to the inkwell, he sat back in his chair and laced his fingers. "Daughter." He offered the word like a bone to a dog, and the hairs on the back of her neck stood on end.

Don't let him get to you, she thought to herself. There was no sense in small talk, neither of them had time for it. Best to get straight to the point.

"I hear you and Tonas are going on a trip," she said as casually as she could.

"It's not a trip, Yanara," he snapped. "We will be conducting important domestic and foreign trade talks, not indulging in some sort of fisherman's holiday."

Damn, got him fired up already.

"Sorry, I didn't mean to trivialise it." She tried to force a smile, to which Osran narrowed his eyes.

"What do you want?"

No sense in putting it off.

"I want to come with you," she said matter-of-factly. *There, take that you miserable old bastard.*

He stared at her for a moment, then shook his head. "You must be joking. You've never taken an interest in my business, and I can't believe you're thinking of anyone but yourself by asking this."

You're not wrong, old man.

"I'm not interested in your business. I've never left Selathar, and it's been years since I've even left Kyir. I'm losing my mind here, and I need to see some other places."

There was no deception in what she said. Whilst she left the Keep occasionally, it had been at least four years since she'd left the town, and even that had only been to Manar. Situated to the northwest, it sat in the middle of swamplands, and hadn't exactly resonated with her sense of natural beauty.

Osran grunted and shook his head again.

"No, you would only be a burden. Besides, after you nearly knocked out young Nyar just now I'm hardly in the mood to indulge your fleeting curiosities."

Breathe, just breathe.

"I thought you might say that, so I've got a proposal for you."

He said nothing, staring at her with those cold eyes.

"If you take me with you, I'll stop turning away suitors. I'll marry whoever you want me to."

"Even Nyar?"

"Except Nyar. To be honest I doubt you could convince him to come back. Oh, but not until after we get back. I'm not getting married before we go and then having my husband forbid it."

Osran stood up and walked over to his window. The sun was beginning to set on the horizon, causing a red haze to shine around his form. "Agreed," he said eventually. "You will accompany us to Akhatar and every point we stop along the way. You will conduct yourself properly, or I will send you straight home. Should you manage to make it to the end of our trip without embarrassing me and shaming our House, I will allow you to marry the suitor of your choice. If you have not chosen after the third suitor, I will choose for you."

He turned and walked back over to the desk, resuming his seat. "Do we have an agreement?" he asked.

"Yes." *You gullible old fool.*

"Good. Now leave me, I have work to do."

Smiling to herself, Yanara turned and left the study, gently shutting the door behind her. It was a big thing, what she had promised him. Agreeing to marry after all this time should keep him on side for a time.

Long enough at least for her to disappear at the other end of their journey.

CHAPTER SEVEN

NAIDAR TALET WAS not a man of strong character, Tonas decided as he sat across the table from him in the Great Hall. A pale man not much older than his own son, he had the look of an excitable child about to attempt something clearly beyond him.

The rumours about his father despising him could well be true. That business with Chessa certainly adds credence to the idea.

Tonas struggled to imagine not wanting to know his own son, though Deran was a fine man and had rarely given him cause for concern, let alone disdain.

Yanara was sat next to Tonas, with an imperious expression on her face and a cup of wine in her hand. She had been instrumental in bringing the two Houses to the negotiating table, but he suspected that her reasons for doing so were not purely for the benefit of House Vasso.

Clearing his throat, Tonas rose from his seat, shortly followed by the others at the table. "My lord Naidar," he said with a bow. "As Houselord Vasso, I welcome you to my home in the spirit of cooperation and friendship. You already know my sister, the Lady Yanara, who has worked hard to bring our two Houses together at this table."

"It is an honour to be received by you, my lord," Naidar replied, returning the bow. "And on behalf of all of House Talet, please accept my sincerest condolences on the passing of your father. He was a good man, and his faith in these negotiations was a source of reassurance to us. This is a momentous day in the history of our Houses. The future will be written here."

An excitable man indeed, Tonas thought.

"It is of course a pleasure to see you again, Lady Yanara," Naidar continued. "Your grace and beauty are matched only by your intellect and wit."

Yanara shifted in her seat, clearly uncomfortable. "Thank you, my lord," she replied. "I trust your journey was without incident."

"It was indeed, my lady, though it made for a dull trip if I'm being honest!" Naivar chuckled. "May I introduce our advisor, Javin? He has served my House faithfully, and I welcome his guidance during these negotiations."

The Talet advisor Javin remained silent, though Tonas got the distinct impression that he did not have a higher opinion of Naidar than anyone else in the room.

"Please be seated, all," Tonas said. "I would like to open these negotiations with the subject of trade. I understand that House Talet has again expressed an interest in opening a trade agreement with our House?"

Naidar looked at Javin, who nodded slightly, before replying. "Not exactly, my lord. For many years, our beloved Manar has been caught in an unfortunate geographical quandry between Kyir in the south and Evellim in the north. You have an extant trade route which runs through our land, yet due to your refusal to open trade with us, we are forced to impose tolls on that trade route to generate income."

"We have made this clear on several occasions," Tonas replied. "A trade agreement between Kyir and Manar carries no benefit for us. The only goods you have for export are your grain, which we are already producing in ample quantity."

That was only part of the issue. House Talet had managed to reduce the cost of Manar grain well below that of Kyir. If Tonas allowed cheap grain to flood the markets of Kyir, the livelihoods of countless Kyir farmers would be at risk. It was the main reason they tolerated the tolls imposed by House Talet.

"You misunderstand, my lord," Naidar said. "House Talet accepts the facts as you have stated them. That is why we are willing to forego the tolls for Vasso caravans travelling through our land."

This was unexpected, Tonas thought. The tolls had been in place for many years, and though not extortionate, they still provided a steady stream of funds to House Talet. Had they found an alternative source of income? "That is indeed a generous offer, my lord Naidar. What do you ask for in return?"

Javin leaned in to whisper in Naidar's ear, who swallowed nervously before responding. "We request trade rights with Shas-Ur."

Tonas was stunned. It was an established fact amongst all Houselords that House Vasso retained exclusive trade rights with Shas-Ur, owing to the relationship established between their leaders and the first Houselord, Viuhn Vasso.

Viuhn had ruled as Houselord Vasso some one hundred and eighty years ago, before the First Realm War. In those days, House Vasso was a minor player amongst the other Selathi Houses, with next to no influence over its neighbours. Tensions had been rising between the Houses for a number of years, and most advisors predicted that war was not far off.

It was on an autumn morning that Viuhn had been on a hunting expedition at the foot of the mountains that bordered Shas-Ur, when he came across a young Shas-Uri slumped at the base of a tree. It turned out the man had been a prince, or at least their closest equivalent. Shas-Uri society was something of a mystery to the Selai.

The prince had suffered wounds in a wolf attack, and Viuhn ordered his companions to help the man. That act of compassion had laid the foundations for a dialogue with Shas-Ur, and that dialogue soon developed into a trade agreement which provided House Vasso with exceptional credibility amongst the other Houses. After the Last Realm War, the Senate had agreed that House Vasso would retain exclusive trade rights with the Shas-Uri, as it was their ancestor who had made it possible.

Tonas was not about to yield that privilege to a House who had not earned the right to trade with the Shas-Ur. "Lord Naidar, forgive me but that is simply not possible. The Shas-Uri are very particular about who they trade with, and we have held that agreement with them for nearly two hundred years."

"I understand that my Lord, but all we are asking for is the right to approach them. Surely you can at least grant us an opportunity to meet with their representatives?"

Something wasn't right here. The Talets had a guaranteed income from the tolls they imposed on the trade caravans. Naidar claimed they were willing to sacrifice a full half of those tolls just for the chance to meet with the Shas-Uri trade masters. By any degree of negotiation, House Talet was yielding far more than they should be at the table.

Yanara spoke up. "My lord Naidar, at the risk of seeming ungrateful, I must ask why you are willing to offer a deal that is clearly more favourable to our House than it is to yours?"

"Risks must be taken sometimes, my lady. This is an opportunity we believe will benefit our House, and I would point out that there is no risk to House Vasso."

"There is every risk, young Talet," Tonas interjected. "If Shas-Ur agrees a trade meeting on our recommendation and your House conducts itself improperly, it could damage the relationship we have had with the Shas-Uri for over a hundred and fifty years. I may have only yesterday assumed the mantle of Houselord Vasso, but do not make the mistake of thinking I am about to throw away everything my father worked to maintain."

Naidar slammed his hands down on the table and opened his mouth as if to confront Tonas, but Javin interrupted before he could make a sound. "My lords, my lady," he said with a voice like sand. "Perhaps this would be a beneficial time to adjourn and allow us to cool our heads. Might I suggest Lord Naidar and I retire to the guest quarters, and we reconvene at an hour of Lord Tonas' choosing?"

Clamping his mouth shut, Naidar rose from his chair and strode out of the Great Hall. Javin shook his head. "I must apologise for the young Lord's behaviour, Lord Tonas. He is a passionate man, but does not know how to temper his emotions."

Tonas eyed Javin with suspicion. He was clearly the real danger here, not Naidar with his immature ramblings. "You are wise, sir. I will send for you when I have considered the proposal fully." Tonas and Javin rose from their seats and bowed.

As the advisor departed the hall, Yanara sipped her wine.

"Things seem to be going well, brother."

* * *

WHEN THE NEGOTIATIONS resumed later that day, Tonas had hoped they would be able to make at least some progress beyond discussion of House Talet's absurd trade proposal. Alas, every time he attempted to move the talks on to other matters, the foolish young Naidar stubbornly refused. Each and every point Tonas made was angrily countered by the young lordling, and by the time the sun began to set even Javin was beginning to lose his composure.

"I cannot believe you are so obstinate as to refuse us a simple request in exchange for free trade across our territory!" Naidar screamed across the table at Tonas. "So much for the wisdom of House Vasso."

"That is enough, my Lord," Javin said firmly. "Do you think the reputation of House Talet is served by your childish tantrums?"

"How dare you!?" Naidar said angrily. He pushed Javin away, almost causing him to topple over his chair. "I am the firstborn son of House Talet! You do not speak to me like that!"

It was a pitiful sight, Tonas thought to himself as the Talet guards struggled to pull the lord away from his advisor. For an heir like Naidar to conduct themselves in such a manner demonstrated that Imdan Talet had neglected to instruct his son in the art of, well, anything. The boy had no patience, no decorum, and no concept of the damage just a few poorly chosen words could have on the relationship between Houses.

These negotiations were failing. It seemed there was no way that an agreement could be reached whilst the issue of trade remained unresolved.

Until Yanara spoke up. "My lords, a moment. Perhaps there is a compromise to be found here, between the passion of House Talet and the pride of House Vasso? Please, Lord Naidar, would you be seated?"

As she spoke, Naidar's anger seemed to melt away like ice under a torch. Strange that her words had such a noticeable and sudden effect on him, Tonas thought. Was there more to their relationship than the discussions she had been conducting on House Vasso's behalf?

"Of course, my lady," Naidar replied. Adjusting his coat, he resumed his seat at the table. Javin did the same, though there was a noticeable gap between him and the young Talet this time.

Smiling, Yanara rose from her seat and began to walk slowly around the table towards Naidar and Javin. "My lords will appreciate the position that House Vasso finds itself in," she said, slowly running her fingers along the edge of the table. "We are responsible for the sole interaction between the nations of Selathar and Shas-Ur. We conduct trade that is rooted in agreements that were made by our forefathers, and these agreements are based on honour and mutual respect. Everything depends upon maintaining that respect, and the slightest tremor could undo all we have achieved in the last two hundred years with the Shas-Uri. Surely the firstborn son of Imdan Talet can understand this?"

Naidar look unsettled, but eventually nodded.

"Might I also assume," Yanara continued as she walked behind the Talet representatives, "that your desire for such a venture is based upon the opportunity for trade, rather than a diplomatic relationship with our neighbours?"

Tonas suppressed a smile. This was a clever question for Yanara to put to the young Talet. The relationship that House Vasso had with the Shas-Uri was not so much about the financial benefit as it was the prestige of being the sole family permitted to interact with them. All other Houses had agreed to this decades ago, and it was understood that no other House would attempt to undermine that relationship. By posing this question, Yanara was forcing Naidar to either admit any underlying agenda that House Talet might have, or to limit himself to reaching an agreement purely based on the benefit of coin.

Across the table, Naidar was clenching his jaw. "My lady assumes correctly," he said through gritted teeth.

Yanara smiled in the way she always did when she was winning. The same way she used to when they were young. At that moment, Tonas realized he hadn't seen her smile like that since they were children. "Then might I suggest an alternative arrangement?" She stood at the head of the table, her hands resting on the back of the chair before her. "House Talet will maintain its generous offer to lift the tolls on Vasso caravans, be they heading to or from Evellim."

"And in return?" Naidar eyed her with trepidation.

"With the permission of my brother, in return House Vasso will conduct trade on behalf of House Talet. We will receive your goods for trade and transport them across the border to Shas-Ur. We will trade them under our own name, and return any coin made to you without the burden of taxes. This will require an unprecedented level of trust between our two Houses, but is faith not the start of any good relationship?"

Silence hung over the Great Hall, her last words hanging in the air. This was a good deal for House Vasso. Tonas had the opportunity to conduct free trade with Evellim, and all they had to do was trade goods from Manar on behalf of House Talet. Naidar had to accept the deal or risk returning home empty handed, which his father would not take lightly.

But there was something about all this that left him on edge. A feeling of mistrust, perhaps? But towards who, he could not say. He could not throw away this opportunity for the House based purely on a hunch. If he could not reconcile his feelings, he would have to ignore them.

Clearing his throat, Tonas rose from his seat and faced the Talet delegation. "I would find this acceptable. Lord Naidar, do you agree to these terms?"

Naidar looked at Javin, who leant in and whispered in his ear. The two exchanged a few hushed comments, before he stood and bowed to Tonas. "My lord, on behalf of House Talet, it would be my honour to accept your proposal. I trust we can overlook my…indiscretion, and move forward in the spirit in which Lady Yanara first approached us."

Yanara smiled at him, and raised her arms in response as though offering an embrace. Tonas had seen that pose before, many years previously, but he could not recall where or who from. "Then it seems we have an agreement, my lords," she said, victory rich in her voice. "It would be a shame to let this momentum go to waste, so might I suggest we attempt to conclude these negotiations before dinner? I know of at least three other outstanding matters that warrant further discussion."

Returning to her seat, Yanara poured herself a cup of wine. She had a smug look on her face, and in that moment Tonas knew that she was going to be insufferable from now on. With Father gone, her rebellious streak would surface once again, and life as Houselord Vasso was going to be anything but simple.

* * *

THE REMAINDER OF the negotiations had proceeded far better after the trade compromise. With some occasional spurring from Yanara, they had managed to reach agreements on mutual defence against Lharasan raiders and the pirates that roamed the Sea of Tears, joint scientific and archaeological expeditions, and some unprecedented but curious notion about sending children to each other's schools.

After the final discussions had concluded, Tonas had spoken for a few moments about their agreement and their hopes for the future. Naidar had followed this by speaking at length about anything that seemed to be entering his mind, and it wasn't until Javin interrupted him again that he eventually sat down. Not counting the madman who had accosted him in the street some weeks previously raving about how his shoes were alive, Tonas had never met a man who enjoyed the sound of his own voice so much.

As they left the Great Hall, Tonas gestured for Yanara to remain. "Sister, I owe you my thanks," he admitted.

Yanara eyed him with a cold look, but remained silent.

"I know we've had our differences, but if it weren't for you then these talks would never have been possible. You went out of your way to conduct the initial talks on your own, relieving the burden on myself and Father. I know he would have been proud of what you helped us to accomplish today."

At those words, Yanara's eye narrowed. "Proud? Don't make me laugh, *brother*." She almost snarled the word at him. "Osran was never proud of me, not in life and certainly not in death. You made sure of that at every possible moment, and now you patronise me by offering me words of gratitude?"

She walked over to one of the grand, stained glass windows that ran along the length of the Great Hall's southern wall. It depicted an old man, clad in crimson robes and holding a golden staff with a green jewel mounted on the top. The man had two faces, one on each side of his head. One was young and fair, wearing a pleasant expression as he looked down upon upon a group of serfs who were raising their hands in adoration. The other face was aged and ugly, and surveyed a wasteland littered with ash and bones.

"I may have suffered your duplicity all these years, but I assure you the people will not. Any failings on your part will be magnified tenfold simply because you are Houselord, and believe me, I will not be there to save you."

Tonas, realised he was clenching his jaw, relaxed and took a deep breath. "If you resent Father and I that much, why did you arrange these negotiations for us?"

"For you!?" Yanara wheeled about and locked eyes with him. "Your hubris is truly boundless. I didn't do this for you, or Osran, or your miserable progeny. I did this for House Vasso, to ensure we continue to be a family to be reckoned with. Yours is not the only line that has to suffer the consequences of your actions and decisions."

Tonas rose from his seat and walked over to Yanara. He could almost see the tension in her muscles, and for a moment he went to rest his hand on her shoulder. As he did, something surged through him, like a primal fear one would experience when putting their hand near a naked flame.

Stepping away, he clasped his hands behind his back and steeled himself for the exchange.

"Yanara, I will concede that perhaps I have not been as good a brother as I could have been. My life has been spent preparing to succeed Father, and I will not apologise for that. The people deserve a prepared and learned Houselord, and I have endeavoured to be that man. I cannot apologise on Father's behalf, but I would hope you could have found it in your heart to forgive him now that he has passed."

"I will never forgive him," Yanara said quietly, her voice trembling. "Nor will I forgive you. What the two of you did to me has haunted me every night for the last thirteen years. I was shunned, left to raise my daughter without so much as a glance from her grandfather or uncle." She raised her hand to her face and wiped a tear from her eye. "Forgiveness is earned, Tonas. Nothing you have done since we returned from Akhatar can ever make up for what you took from me. That loss can never be repaid."

Turning away, she walked to the entrance of the Great Hall, stopping at the doorway.

"Fear not, brother," she said. The tone of her voice was once more smooth, like velvet. "Whilst our relationship may be beyond repair, you can be sure that I remain loyal to House Vasso.

Everything I do, everything I have done, is for this House."

And then she was gone, leaving Tonas alone in the Great Hall with that peculiar feeling rising in his stomach again as the setting sun shone warmly through the stained glass.

A shadow stirred in the bushes outside.

CHAPTER EIGHT

Fourteen years ago

"THAT," SAID YANARA in a disgusted tone, "was the single most vile thing I have ever experienced. How do those men do that for months at a time?"

She brushed herself down as she disembarked the transport ship, flicking wooden splinters off her dress. After a voyage lasting several days, they had finally arrived at the docks of Laktam, the primary trade hub of Akhatar on its western cost.

On the jetty ahead, Tonas frowned at her. "These men work harder than you do, sister. Given that they've spent the last few days listening to nothing but your whining, the least you can do is show a bit of respect for their profession."

Scowling at him, Yanara looked back at the crew who were currently jeering at her from the deck. They were making lewd gestures and shouting incomprehensibly in their rough voices, though she was sure she could make out references to her virginity.

"You mean those pigs?" she snorted, turning back to Tonas. "They're not even worth my air." Stepping off the gangway and onto the jetty alongside him, she took a moment to survey the city before her.

Laktam was built into the side of a vast cliff as tall as a mountain. Criss-crossing roadways were cut into the face of the cliff, taking wagons and carts up and over the top. The city itself was made up of countless ivory coloured buildings of varying shapes and sizes, piled up against the cliff like rubbish in an alley.

Despite this haphazard placement, the buildings themselves were all strikingly beautiful. The sun reflected off the surfaces, making the whole city appear as though it were on fire. It was a stark contrast from Kyir, which consisted mostly of wooden structures sitting amongst vast rolling wheat fields.

"Impressed?" Osran's voice sounded from right behind Yanara, making her jump.

"It's certainly diffcrent," she conceded, determined not to give him the satisfaction of seeing her speechless. "How old is the city?"

"The reports vary. Akhani scholars maintain that the city is over three thousand years old, but our own historians have found no evidence of its existence that far back." He paused, scratching his beard. "Of course, in the interests of diplomacy we do not discuss such discrepancies at times like this. I require your discretion in this matter."

Yanara sighed. "Of course."

"Oh, and you must address me as Father whilst we're here. I won't have our…differences making our hosts uncomfortable."

"Who are our hosts?" Yanara asked, suppressing an urge to shiver.

"It appears we'll be meeting them soon," Osran said, pointing to a group approaching them from the end of the jetty.

A retinue of armoured soldiers marched towards them from the other end of the jetty, each in perfect step with the other. Yanara was taken aback, not only at how ornate their armour was but also at how much of it they were wearing. Each man was decked head to toe in layers of overlapping black plate armour with silver trims and flourishes, and white cloaks hung down their backs. Their helmets covered their faces completely, with only the smallest eye slits granting them vision. Yanara was no military tactician, but it certainly seemed to be an armour designed for intimidation, and not effective combat.

At the head of the retinue was a woman dressed in black and yellow robes. An odd combination, Yanara thought, but then these were strange people in a strange land. She'd been told in her youth that the Akhanu were a strange looking people. Her brothers had spun tales of how they looked like pale ghosts, and their hair was black like tar. She'd looked forward to seeing an Akhan one day, more out of curiosity than anything. This woman had the trademark pale skin and black hair of the Akhanu; however, combined with her sharp features and pointed nose it gave her a decidedly unpleasant appearance.

Osran bowed slightly as the group stopped in front of them, with Tonas following suit. Yanara simply stood in awe until Osran gave her a sharp look, prompting her to bow as well. The woman returned the bow before returning to a standing position and spreading her arms theatrically.

"My Lord Osran Vasso. I am Wissalla, Speaker for the Regent of Laktam, the honourable Ainnarus Re'Shennu. On behalf of the Regent, allow me to welcome you to our magnificent city."

"Speaker Wisalla," Osran replied, "my children and I are honoured by your welcome. We have travelled far to do business with your Regent and seek leave to enter his home."

Yanara suppressed a laugh and leant in to Tonas. "Are they for real?" she whispered. "It's like watching bad theatre."

Tonas sighed and shook his head. "The Akhanu are an exceptionally proud people," he said, matching her hushed tone. "They insist on observing correct protocol when meeting for the first time and expect the same from their guests. Father has been engaging with Akhani delegates for years, so it's second nature to him. We just need to do as we're told and not upset anyone."

Easier said than done, thought Yanara. *That seems to be my specialty.*

"Allow me to introduce my children," Osran was saying with a gesture. "My firstborn son and heir, Tonas Vasso."

Tonas bowed to Wissalla but said nothing.

"And this," Osran continued, "is my daughter, Yanara."

Suppressing a grimace, Yanara bowed slightly.

Not worthy of the family name when being introduced, Father? No surprises there.

"It is an honour to receive you all," the speaker replied. "If I might escort you to the palace, the Regent and his sons are eager to meet you."

Stepping back from them, Wissalla clapped her hands twice and a group of attendants appeared from behind the guards to collect their belongings, before disappearing ahead of the delegation.

As their group left the jetty and began the long winding walk through the streets of Laktam towards the palace, Yanara noticed something peculiar. Whilst a good number of the Akhanu were working, none of them were of a class lower than the average merchant. Looking down side streets, she saw no sign of beggars, thieves or whores, and the city was remarkably clean. No mud in the streets, or filth in the gutters.

Turning to Osran and opening her mouth, Yanara felt a pinch on her arm before she could say anything.

"Whatever you were about to ask, don't even think about it," Tonas chided her quietly, a dark expression creeping onto his face. "Father told you not to cause a fuss."

"I don't understand," she replied under her breath. Then, raising her voice before Tonas could stop her, she continued. "I was only going to ask where all the poor are."

She knew instantly that she had made a mistake, as Tonas' hand tightened on her arm and Osran stopped dead in his tracks. As he turned to look at her, she recoiled at the intense look in his eyes.

"Yanara, what did I just say!?" Tonas said angrily. "Speaker Wissalla, please forgive my sister's rudeness."

"It is quite all right, my lord Tonas." Wissalla replied with a smile. "Where once the nation of Akhatar was made to feel ashamed of its practices, we have come to realise in recent years that we need not justify ourselves, even to our friends."

What does she mean?

"The reason our streets are so clean and free from…undesirables, is because they simply do not exist," she stated matter-of-factly. "Laktam, like all other Akhani cities, has only good and loyal citizens."

"How can that be?" Yanara asked. "What about those who fall on hard times or break the law?"

"As I said, my lady," Wissalla replied, "they do not exist. Such individuals have no place in our glorious nation."

Wait, is she saying what I think she's saying?

"Yanara," Osran said with a firm voice. "You will stop asking questions this instant."

"As you say…Father."

Narrowing his eyes at her, Osran continued. "Speaker Wissalla, might I ask that you do not indulge my daughter's curiosity any further? She has neither the tongue nor temperament for diplomacy, and I would rather not tarnish our discussions with her misguided choice of words."

"Of course, my lord," Wissalla replied. "If you will continue to follow me, we are nearly at the palace."

Her face flushing red in humiliation, Yanara clenched her jaw and stepped back from the group. Once again, Osran had made her feel small and insignificant. She had assumed that accompanying him on this trip might have earned her some favour in his eyes.

I guess I assumed wrong. Hateful man.

As they continued on, Yanara silently decided that it was probably better to say as little as possible for the remainder of their time there. After all, she didn't have to interact with the world to be able to see it.

* * *

THE THRONE ROOM of the palace was the most outlandish scene Yanara had ever laid eyes upon. The walls on either side of them were lined with tables piled high with all manner of exotic fruits, breads and fountains gushing a clear liquid that she strongly suspected was not water. The floor was covered in intricate floral designs which merged at the dais and fed into bronze vines that crept up either side of the ornate throne.

Upon the throne was sat a small, elderly man in equally extravagant robes, though his were not black and yellow like Wissalla's. He wore pure white robes with gold pauldrons over the shoulders, from which hung small gold chains that fell in loops over his chest and arms. His presumably once black hair was now dark grey with flecks of white in it, and his pale skin was almost translucent in his old age. His eyes were completely black, including where the whites of his eyeballs should have been. All in all, he was a very unsettling sight to Yanara.

"My lord Osran," Wissalla said loudly, adopting the same ridiculous pose she had greeted them with down on the jetty. "Please allow me to introduce the honourable Ainnarus Re'Shennu, Regent of Laktam and the King's own Voice of the South."

Yanara rolled her eyes, desperately trying not to burst out laughing at the overstated extravagance of it all. She was more than willing to accept the alternative customs of other lands and peoples, but the Akhanu just acted like they were in one long, badly written play.

"Regent," Osran was replying. "Your welcome does me great honour."

"As does your presence in my home, Lord Osran," Ainnarus said as he rose from his throne with an energy that belied his age. For a seemingly old man, he had no difficult moving around. "Now, come here my old friend."

As the two men embraced, Yanara felt a stab of jealousy.

This decrepit old man earns a hug, but I can barely get Osran to look at me?

She felt anger rising in her heart, accompanied by a prickling sensation on her skin. What was that?

"Sister," Tonas said as he grasped her arm. Looking down, she saw her fist was clenched, and she took a deep breath. She wouldn't let Osran get to her like this, not again.

"Thank you, brother," she said, squirming out of his grip. "I'll be fine. Go stand with Father. I'm sure he'll want to introduce you."

Ignoring the look of pity on his face, Yanara walked over to one of the tables and began examining the various foods on offer. As she picked up a red fruit with yellow streaks, she noticed something peculiar about the weight and texture of it. It was heavier than most other fruits, and the skin had a strange grain to it which contrasted with the glossy red colouring.

It was wood.

She looked around at the room to see if anyone was paying attention to her. Ainnarus was introducing his firstborn son, Innis, to Tonas. Turning back to the table, she picked up another item, this time green. That fruit, and every other item of what appeared to be food on the table was made of carved, painted wood. There was nothing edible in the room, and Yanara fought to keep her surprise hidden.

"Appearances can be deceiving, my lady."

The male voice from behind her made Yanara jump, and she wheeled around with a face like thunder to confront the intruder into her personal space. The man who smiled back at her, however, caught her completely off guard.

His skin was pale, but beautiful like porcelain, free from blemishes, scars or flushing. He had black hair, like all Akhan, but it wasn't greasy like tar. It was like the night, deep and dashed with occasional streaks of dark blue and purple.

He wore black trousers under a white and grey tunic, also with pauldrons like Ainnarus except his were cast in silver with matching chains.

More than anything else, she had found herself noticing his eyes. In contrast to her own, which were a deep hazel, his were a deep emerald green. She'd never seen anything like it before, and for the first time in her life she'd been lost for words.

Smiling at her again, the man took the fruit from her hands and tossed it up in the air, catching it with his other hand. "You see, here in Akhatar we aren't blessed with fertile lands like you are in Selathar. We import what we can, but even the ruling class can't afford to be wasteful at the expense of the people. Most don't have the same keen eye that you have."

Finding her confidence again, Yanara composed herself and locked eyes with the handsome man who had so skilfully disarmed her. "Forgive me. I am not familiar with Akhani customs, but where I come from it's generally considered polite to introduce yourself to a lady before engaging her in conversation."

The man opened his mouth to reply, but was interrupted by a voice from across the room.

"Ah, and I see your daughter has already met my other son. Firrus, won't you bring the young lady over?"

Yanara looked at him in surprise. "Firrus?"

"Yes, my apologies. My lady, allow me to introduce myself. I am Firrus Re'Shennu, secondborn son of the Regent," he said, taking her hand and planting a kiss on the back of it. "And might I add, it is my pleasure and honour to meet you."

She felt her heart skip a beat and her face flush all in the same moment, and once again she was lost for words. The touch of his lips on her skin set her nerves on fire, and she felt her hand clench again. He looked up at her again and smiled, and she smiled back nervously.

Well, here's your dashing prince. Now what?

CHAPTER NINE

CHESSA WATCHED AS the twins ran around their new chamber, Corin chasing Vishki with a spider he had plucked from underneath the dresser. Osran's death had resulted in some movement of family members between rooms, with Tonas and Ciloni moving into the Houselord's chambers at the end of the hallway. This had allowed Deran to move into the heir's chambers which meant Yanara and Sima could move into his old chamber.

As a result of all these moves, a smaller chamber had been left free next door to Deran, and the decision had been taken to move the twins in there. Tonas had originally offered for Sima to have it as her own, but Yanara had refused to be separated from her daughter.

"My daughter stays with me, always," she had said to Tonas with a bitter edge to her voice.

After a brief heated exchange, the matter had been dropped and the twins had been shown the room, much to their delight. They had never had their own space before, and the dose of independence had addled their brains somewhat.

Of course, in another five or six years they'll start going through the change and have to be separated, but we can deal with that when the time comes, I suppose.

Chessa chuckled to herself as she imagined what the twins would be like as they entered adolescence. She had little experience with children other than those two, but she knew that they were as unpredictable as they were individual. There was every chance their personalities could swing the other direction, and Corin could become the reserved, thoughtful one whilst Vishki became a wild child.

As she plucked Corin off the windowsill where he was perched precariously, she wondered whether she would ever have children of her own. Truth be told, her oath to House Vasso left her unable to commit to anything or anyone else. Even if she did meet someone else, she would be reliant on Tonas releasing her from her oath voluntarily. Perhaps he would if Deran…

Her face flushed red at the thought of the twins' father, and she put Corin down and ushered him away. These feelings she had for Deran were not healthy and conflicted with her duty to the rest of the family. Whilst she longed to explore those feelings, she was still unsure if Deran shared them. Perhaps…

No! Enough of this, you stupid woman.

Chiding herself for her self-indulgence, she looked up to see Deran entering the room. He looked as dashing and alluring as ever, and she turned away as her face reddened once more. *In the name of the Shattered Child, why is this happening to me now?*

"Good afternoon, Chessa. I trust the twins are enjoying their new accommodation?"

"It would seem so, my lord. Though I may have to put barbed wire on the windowsill if young Master Corin doesn't stop climbing on it." She gave a mischievous wink at the boy, who looked at her in fear for a moment before realising she was teasing him. He ran over and playfully slapped her on the leg.

"Corin!" Deran exclaimed. "What have I told you about hitting?"

The boy stopped, looking at the floor bashfully. "You said not to hit people. Don't hit people, and really don't hit people bigger than me."

"Correct. Now what do you say?"

Corin looked up at Chessa with an expression of genuine sorrow, and for a moment her heart wrenched. She cared about the children, probably more than she should do.

"Sorry," Corin apologised. "I won't hit you again."

Settling onto her knees in front of him, Chessa grasped his shoulders. "You promise?"

"I promise."

"Good boy," she said warmly, giving him a hug. "Now, why don't you go with your sister and pick some flowers from the courtyard. This room needs some warmth, and there's an empty vase on the dresser."

Grinning from ear to ear, Corin pulled back and looked at her. She was shocked to see genuine love in his eyes, but what came next took her completely by surprise.

"Okay Mama!" he said as he grabbed Vishki's wrist and dragged her out of the room.

Chessa simply knelt where she was, staring at the patterns on the rug in front of her.

Mama. He called me Mama.

"Chessa?" Deran asked timidly.

Tears began to stream down her face, and she angrily wiped them away with a cloth from her pocket. This was exactly what she had hoped to avoid, and yet it had happened anyway. How could she protect the entire family if she was concerned about the children above all others?

She stood to leave, trying not to make eye contact with Deran, but as she moved towards the door he caught her arm.

"Chessa, please stay." The look in his eyes was one of pain, almost desperation.

"My lord, please let me go," she pleaded. "I can't do this, not now."

Deran's grip loosened slightly, and she took the opportunity to free herself and escape through the door and into the hallway. Pulling the door shut behind her, she took a moment to compose herself and bury those feelings.

Now is not the time for this, Chessa.

Shaking her head, she adjusted her clothing and made to step towards the Great Hall when she heard arguing coming from Yanara's chambers opposite. She assumed Sima was being difficult again, but when she listened more carefully she could hear a man's voice.

It was Naidar.

What is he doing in Yanara's chambers? Aside from the fact that it's rather improper for a male guest to be in a lady's private chambers, he shouldn't have any business in there.

Stealing a quick glance to see if anyone was around, Chessa stepped closer to the door. She was surprised that the sound was so muffled. After all, the door was only wood and there were gaps around the door where it did not quite fit in the frame. She was able to make out a few words, however.

"…ridiculous…cannot…me…agree…"

That was Yanara. What could they be talking about?

"…agreement…sense…us…rescinded."

Naidar sounded frustrated, as though he was being rejected. That would make sense, as Yanara never demonstrated any interest in men. Her only love was for her daughter.

"OUT!"

That was clear enough. Chessa instinctively stepped back a few feet as footsteps indicated that someone was approaching the door, but instead of walking away she walked towards the door again.

As Naidar exited the room, he almost crashed into her. "Out of my way, foolish woman!" He stormed off towards the Entrance Hall, leaving Chessa stood outside Yanara's chamber.

The two women exchanged suspicious glances for a moment, before Chessa bowed slightly. "My lady." She did not wait for a reply, wheeling about and following Naidar down the hallway.

What is going on?

* * *

A CHEER ROSE in the Great Hall as one of the guests fell off the table in a drunken stupor. Whilst such behaviour was not commonly tolerated in Vasso Keep, Chessa had watched Naidar spend the better part of the last three hours goading the Vasso courtiers into taking part in bets and drinking games. Though she would never admit it, she enjoyed the atmosphere and revelry of a feast, particularly when it gave her the chance to unwind with the men under her command.

Presently a fight broke out between a small group in the corner, and Chessa nodded to the guards nearby to break it up. Part of her job this evening was to keep things in order whilst still allowing for the usual drunken antics.

Tonas and Ciloni were sat at the head table, observing the feast with diplomatic smiles on their faces. Yanara and Sima were seated next to Ciloni, as was the tradition. Women of the house were expected to entertain each other at feasts, though Ciloni and Yanara did not get on and were exchanging only the briefest of words. Frankly, there wasn't anybody in the family that Yanara got on with.

On Tonas' left side was Naidar, beyond drunk and continuing to make a fool of himself. Curiously, Javin was nowhere to be seen. Chessa had expected him to be sat next to Naidar to keep him in check, but she hadn't seen him since the end of the negotiations earlier that day.

Peculiar. Perhaps I should have one of the guards search for him.

Deran was sat on the other side of Naidar, looking distinctly uncomfortable at the man's behaviour. He had never been one for excessive drinking. She'd kept her distance from Deran that evening by sitting at the top end of a table at the opposite side of the hall near Yanara, afraid that alcohol would loosen her tongue and damage their relationship even further. The incident in the twins' chamber earlier had shaken her, and she knew that at some point she would have to face Deran and talk about it. The twins had been sent to bed as soon as the first cup was broken, with a guard posted outside their chamber for protection, in addition to the four guards assigned to seal off the hallway leading to the family chambers.

"Ladies and gentlemen!" Naidar shouted across the hall as he clambered to his feet. Tonas looked up at him with a concerned expression on his face, and then at Chessa. Nodding in respect, she exchanged a few subtle eye movements with the guards behind the head table, who quietly positioned themselves to remove the Talet heir if he got out of control.

"What an auspicious occasion this is!" Naidar continued, gesturing with his wine which began to spill over Deran. Chessa watched as he took a deep breath, then wiped himself down and removed himself to another table across from her. An attendant carefully teased the cup out of Naidar's hand, though he didn't seem aggrieved by this.

"Today marks the start of a new chapter between our two Houses," he proclaimed with a mild slur. "For the first time in decades, House Talet will benefit from a new trade agreement with Selathar's neighbours to the south west, the honourable Shas-Uri.

House Vasso will benefit from toll-free trade routes through Talet lands, and together we will boldly venture into a prosperous future for both our Houses!!"

As the guests cheered again, Chessa looked along the head table. Tonas and Ciloni were clapping, though both seemed awkward, and Sima was busy looking at herself in a handheld mirror. Yanara, on the other hand, simply sat there and rolled her eyes. Whether it was Naidar or the wine, she seemed incredibly uninterested in the whole affair.

"But alas," Naidar said suddenly, "what use is prosperity and security without someone special to share it with?"

Chessa noticed Yanara suddenly became rigid in her seat, her eyes wide.

What is he talking about? And why is Yanara suddenly so on edge?

She didn't have to wait long for her answer. Naidar stepped back from the table and walked along to where Yanara was sitting. "My lady Yanara. Since we first met, I have been able to think of nothing else but you. Your beautiful face, your shocking white hair. It is thanks to you that these talks were able to take place, and for that you have won my heart."

He dropped to a knee beside her and took her hand. "Will you do me the honour of marrying me?"

If Naidar's face was the picture of drunken love, then Yanara's was quite the opposite. In fact, Chessa had never seen her look so angry in all the time she had known her. If looks could kill, Naidar would have been a visceral mess on the floor by now.

She watched as Yanara stood from her seat, grabbed Sima by the hand and stormed from the Great Hall. As the two walked past her, Chessa almost thought she could see what looked like smoke trailing behind Yanara. It was probably a trick of the light, however, or maybe some of the candle smoke had clung to her previously.

The Great Hall was silent as the guests watched Yanara leave, then turned to look at Naidar. Chessa considered that he had once again proven himself the fool of House Talet and judging by his earlier behaviour that Tonas had reported to her, he was likely to cause a scene in the next few minutes.

Signalling her guards again, she rose from her seat and approached Naidar. "My lord, might I escort you to your chambers? Some rest, perhaps, will sooth your mood."

Naidar's face contorted in anger, and he raised a hand as if to strike her. But her guards were quicker, and they soon had him restrained, though he continued to put up a fight. Some of the Talet guards nearby made as if to intervene, but Chessa shot them a dangerous glance. "Your lord will not be harmed. Men, please escort the young lord to his chambers."

As Tonas nodded his gratitude to Chessa, she watched as Naidar was dragged from the Great Hall kicking and screaming. Rolling her eyes, she leant in to whisper in the ear of one of the remaining guards. "Make sure there's extra men watching him tonight. Two of yours, two of his. Make sure he is checked on regularly. If last night's behaviour is anything to go by, we don't want the young Lord choking on his own vomit."

The guard nodded and left the Great Hall, taking several men from each House with him. The general chatter began to climb again, and the guests returned to their drinking, though it was a great deal more sombre than before.

Chessa watched as Deran moved back to the head table and sat next to his father. The two of them engaged in quiet conversation, though she saw Deran glance at her occasionally. An uncomfortable feeling rising in her stomach, she got up from the table just as Ciloni approached her from the head table. Chessa bowed before smiling weakly at the older woman,

"Chessa, my dear," Ciloni said as she stepped up to her. "Might I beg your company for a moment?"

"Of course, my lady," Chessa replied.

"Would you step into the courtyard with me?" Ciloni asked with a warm voice. "My words are not for the ears of others."

Puzzled, Chessa nodded and turned to look at Tonas and Deran. Both were still talking in hushed tones, and she heard Ciloni chuckle behind her. "Oh, don't worry about them. They'll be talking for some time. Come."

The two women stepped through the side door into the courtyard and walked towards a bench on the other side. Ciloni took a seat and patted the space next to her.

"I really would rather stand, my lady."

"And I would really rather you sat, dear," Ciloni retorted with a wicked smile. "Surely I'm not that intimidating?"

Sighing, Chessa sat on the other half of the stone bench,

fidgeting uncomfortably. She was not accustomed to situations like this, where the focus was on her.

"Chessa," Ciloni said softly, "how old are you now?"

"Twenty eight, my lady."

"I see." Ciloni looked up at the stars and took a deep breath. "You know, by the time I was your age, I'd already been married for several years and had two sons."

Chessa suppressed a sense of dread. This was exactly the kind of subject she wasn't comfortable discussing. "That's…nice. Were you happy, my lady?"

"Of course not. No woman is ever happy being forced into an arranged marriage. But in time, I grew to love Tonas, and I knew my duty was to support him."

"Duty is important," Chessa agreed.

"That depends, my dear." Ciloni fixed her with a shrewd look. "Does our duty leave us truly fulfilled? Or does it get in the way? Does our duty stop us from pursuing things we otherwise might already possess?"

"My lady, I'm not sure I know what you're getting at."

"Oh you do Chessa, you're just being evasive. I'm talking about your feelings for my son."

Oh no.

"My lady, I…how do you know about that?"

"I may be the wife of a Houselord, but I'm still a woman. I recognise certain behaviours, and it's not difficult to see how you act around Deran."

Chessa began to fidget again. "It's not something I'm really ready to talk about, my lady."

"Tough. We're going to talk about it, because frankly I'm sick of watching the two of you staring at each other like lost puppies."

"My lady?"

"Chessa, it's blatantly obvious to me that you care for one another. The only issue is your own fears and damned self-condemnation. You refuse to entertain the idea of abandoning your oath, and he's so guilt-ridden over the thought of moving on from Giva that he can't bring himself to tell you how he feels. If I'm being perfectly honest, it's boring me."

Chessa sat stunned. She hadn't expected this, least of all from Ciloni. The woman's wit and sharp tongue bit deep, but she had to admit there was truth to all of it. "What should I do?"

"Do you trust me, Chessa?"

"Of course, my lady."

"Then leave it to me. I'll speak with him, but I want you to promise me that you'll follow your heart in this matter, and not that damned oath of yours."

"If it comes to it, then yes my lady, I will. But until that moment comes, I must keep my oath. Your lives are my top priority, no matter what place I hold in this House."

"Of course. Now, shall we go back inside? I believe there is still more joviality to come and enough of your guards are present that you can afford to unwind."

"I really shouldn't, my lady."

"What have we just spoken about? Don't make me order you to have fun."

Chessa sighed, then laughed softly. Was this going to be a recurring theme? "As you say, my lady."

CHAPTER TEN

Fourteen years ago

YANARA CLOSED HER eyes as the warm evening breeze blew gently across her cheek. She was laid with her head in Firrus' lap, enjoying the sensation of his fingers running through her hair and occasionally playing with the dark brown locks. Despite his athletic strength, he had a gentle touch and was careful not to hurt her.

It hadn't been Yanara's plan to meet anyone whilst in Akhatar, especially given her intention to disappear once Osran and Tonas were sufficiently distracted with their negotiations.

She definitely hadn't planned on falling in love with the son of an Akhani regent.

From the moment they had met, Yanara had been caught up in a whirlwind of thoughts and feelings which she'd never experienced before. Firrus was intelligent, considerate, and fiercely protective of her, a combination which had left her unable to think about anything else but him.

He had taken her to the top of the city, where gardens built into the cliff afforded spectacular views of Laktam and the bay at the head of the Tranquil Sea. They had lunched amongst the flowerbeds, and strolled through the menageries.

One evening, they had embarked a boat at the harbour and sailed out into the bay. As the sun had set, Yanara was shocked to see lights in the water.

"What is that?" she had asked.

"It's the creatures in the water. They produce a special chemical in their bodies which lights up and makes beautiful patterns. We don't understand exactly how the chemical does this, but it's considered one of the most beautiful sights around Laktam."

That night they had simply watched the lights dance around the ship, occasionally sharing a tender kiss.

For three months, Firrus had opened Yanara's eyes to a world outside Kyir and Vasso Keep. Every time they did something new, however, she couldn't help but think that one day soon it would end.

"What are you thinking?" Firrus' Akhani accent had a soft, silky edge to it which made her melt every time he spoke.

She turned her head to look at him, almost losing herself in those emerald eyes again. "Just about time and how it always gets away from you. What do you think will happen when it's time for me to leave?"

Firrus laughed, and she sat up from his lap.

"Is something funny?" she demanded with her arms folded across her chest.

"Who says you have to leave?" he chuckled, unfolding her arms and taking her hands in his. "There's no reason that you can't stay here."

"Firrus, I made a promise to my father. I have to marry when I return home. That was the agreement we had in exchange for me being allowed to accompany him."

"The way I see it, you could get married sooner."

She looked at him in confusion for a few moments, then suddenly realised what he was saying. Jumping up from the bench, she stalked to the window shaking her head. "Are you serious?!" she exclaimed, trying not to let the emotion show in her voice. "We've only known each other for three weeks, Firrus. There's no way my father or yours will allow this."

"Why not?" Firrus asked, following her. "Why shouldn't we marry? Better that you marry a man you love, rather than some stranger."

"You're insane." Yanara began to laugh nervously. "There's still so much we don't know about each other. Not to mention the fact that my father will want me to marry a Selathi heir to consolidate his influence back home. We'll never be allowed to do this."

"We never know until we ask," Firrus said with a smile that made her melt. "I suspect my father would agree—he's always been keen to improve relations with Selathar. And by your own admission, this would certainly mean less worry for your father."

Trembling, she ran the scenario over and over in her head. Osran would consider this a rebellious act on her part, as well as a threat to his political and international standing. She was unsure of Akhani customs, and so she had no idea whether Ainnarus would approve the match. If he did, and Osran opposed it, there was the potential for a huge rift in the relationship between Selathar and Akhatar.

As she considered the variables, she realised that none of it mattered to her. She loved Firrus, and she was determined not to let anything get in the way of that.

"I'm scared, Firrus."

"Me too, but at least we can be scared together," he replied, taking her head in his hands. "There's nothing we can't face if we're together."

As he kissed her, she allowed her anxiety to drift away like leaves on the wind. She'd do anything to keep this feeling from ending.

* * *

"OUT OF THE question!" Osran slammed his hand down on the table, causing several goblets to jump where they sat. "I will not allow it! Do you hear me, you wretched girl? I will not allow it!"

It was not an unexpected response on his part, but Yanara had failed to anticipate just how emotive her father would be at the news. Usually a reserved, tempered man, this was a rare outburst of anger from him. She half expected him to begin throwing things in a fit of childish rage.

Fathers had a habit of reacting strangely to news of their daughters getting engaged.

"My lord, please," Firrus said, trying to calm Osran's temper. "I love your daughter very much and want nothing more than to make her happy. Here in Akhatar we take our wedding vows seriously. I assure you I would not ask her to marry me if I did not intend on honouring those vows."

Osran's face was contorted in ways Yanara had never seen

before as he regarded Firrus. It was almost as though he were trying to figure out exactly how he felt about the situation. Or perhaps, trying to construct an excuse in his mind for why she shouldn't marry Firrus.

She watched as Osran took a deep breath and turned back to her. "Are you doing this on purpose?" he asked quietly, a dangerous tone creeping into his voice. "Trying to punish me, or humiliate me? You've known this boy for a matter of weeks, and now you come to me announcing you intend to wed him? Are you trying to undo everything I'm working to achieve here?"

Yanara frowned at her father's argument. He was refusing to allow her to marry someone she'd spent time with and developed feelings for, yet he was perfectly content to marry her off to a relative stranger back home in Selathar. Was it prejudice? No, that wasn't it. He'd been to Akhatar many times, and she'd heard him speak to her brothers with great fondness of the Akhan and their way of life.

So what was it about this engagement that he took issue with?

"Father," Yanara said with a venomous edge to her words, "believe it or not, this is not about you. I can understand how you might think that, given that you think everything in the world revolves around you, but you are wrong. I love Firrus, and I intend to marry him. And if you will not approve, I will simply remain here in Laktam with him. You'll never have to worry about me again, and you can go on acting like you never had a daughter, though I doubt most will notice the difference in your behaviour."

Osran's hand moved so fast that she barely had time to register what was happening as he struck her across the face, causing her to stagger back. Firrus rushed to her side as Tonas pulled his father back.

"How dare you?" Osran said, struggling to control his anger. "I am your father. You will not speak to me with such disrespect!"

"Father!" Tonas exclaimed as he placed himself between the two of them. "Father, you must control yourself. This behaviour is completely out of character for you. For the sake of our relationship with Ainnarus, please calm down."

His words seemed to have some effect, as Osran stopped struggling and hung his head as though in shame.

"Osran," Ainnarus said quietly, "I can see you are upset, but I have no issue with this match. It seems a sensible step, given our working relationship. My son is a fine man, and from what I can see your daughter is a fine woman. Why would you oppose such a marriage?"

"I have my reasons, Ainnarus," Osran replied, not meeting his eye. "Suffice it to say I will not condone this engagement."

He went to turn away, but Firrus grabbed him by the arm. Almost immediately, he released it, realising he had overstepped his mark. "Please," he said desperately, "I will do anything to have your daughter's hand." He kissed Yanara's hand, then turned to face Osran, bracing up with an air of authority that she hadn't seen before. "Osran Vasso, Lord of House Vasso. In accordance with the Old Laws of your country, I respectfully challenge you for the right to your daughter's hand in marriage."

Yanara looked at Firrus in disbelief. Disbelief that he knew anything of the Old Laws of Selathar. Disbelief that he had just challenged her father, a Selathi Houselord, for her hand.

This couldn't be happening.

But then, there was an opportunity here. A challenge under the Old Laws was traditionally settled by combat. Osran was not a fighter, and years of sitting behind a desk drinking wine and eating rich meat had left him physically wanting.

Firrus on the other hand was an accomplished duellist. She had watched him participate in friendly competitions during their time together, and his skill with the blade was something to behold. If he could best Osran in combat, and he likely would, their engagement would be sealed.

"What!?" Tonas exclaimed in disbelief. "You dare challenge my father, the Houselord Vasso? Father, this is incorrigible behaviour."

"You will hold your tongue, Tonas," Osran retorted. He turned to Ainnarus, sighing as he did so. In that moment, with his authority shattered and his energy drained, Yanara saw how old he really was. "The challenge your son makes is valid in accordance with our Old Laws, Ainnarus. What do you say to this?"

The regent bowed his head in quiet contemplation, taking a few moments before responding. "We Akhanu allow our children to make their own mistakes once they are of age. Whilst I do not relish the thought of my own son engaging one of my oldest friends in combat, I am obligated to obey both Selathi and Akhani laws. I have no authority in this matter, even as Regent of Laktam. The challenge has been made, Osran. The decision is up to you."

Osran nodded in respect, then faced Firrus and Yanara once more. "Then I accept your challenge, Firrus Re'Shennu, son of Ainnarus. We will settle this at dawn tomorrow."

He strode from the chamber, leaving Yanara and Firrus alone with Ainnarus.

"I hope you know what you are doing, my son," the old Regent said before following Osran out of the room, leaving the two of them to contemplate what had just happened.

* * *

THEY GATHERED IN the courtyard of Laktam Palace the following morning as the sun was rising, a sombre mood hanging over the group.

Firrus was accompanied by his older brother Innis, with Ainnarus walking behind. Yanara had been forced to walk behind Osran and Tonas.

"You are not part of that family unless Firrus wins his challenge, girl," Osran had said stubbornly.

She had never felt so miserable, not since her father's crushing revelation in the drawing room. Her confidence in Firrus' ability to win the challenge was overshadowed by a sense of foreboding. Something didn't feel right about all this, but she couldn't put a finger on what.

They arrived at the centre of the courtyard, where a gravel circle had been marked with a duelling arena. Two attendants stepped forward, each one carry a sheathed rapier. Firrus picked his up and drew it, inspecting it before carrying out a series of impressive flourishes designed mostly to test the weight and balance, but also to unnerve the opponent. He stepped forward to take his place in the arena and smiled at Yanara.

Osran also drew his rapier, and made a show of inspecting it briefly before he turned around.

And handed it to Tonas.

Wait, what?

Tonas conducted his own inspection, much like Firrus' but with powerful swings instead of complex flourishes. He stepped forward into the arena, taking the spot that should have been for Osran.

"Osran, what is this?" Ainnarus demanded, his hands on his hips.

"The Old Laws do not require that the challenge be settled by the individuals themselves," Osran replied. "I have therefore chosen my firstborn son to duel on my behalf. Firrus is entitled to elect his own champion, of course."

Yanara gritted her teeth. This was a problem, one she hadn't foreseen. Firrus was a skilled swordsman, but Tonas had years of hunting and combat experience behind him. He had a strong arm, possibly stronger than Firrus', and she had seen him best many of the other young men in Kyir.

Firrus' pride meant he would not allow another to fight on his behalf. He would face Tonas himself, putting himself at risk.

Ainnarus was also visibly disturbed. By his own admission Akhani parents did not interfere in their children's affairs after a certain age, yet his instinct to protect his son was at odds with that particular law.

"Father!" Innis pleaded. "There must be something we can do?" Ainnarus's firstborn was frantically looking between the two lords.

"What would you have me do?" Ainnarus demanded of his son. "The challenge is not mine to stop. Firrus must see this through himself, and I will not dispute Selathi law."

He turned to the arena, addressing Tonas and Firrus.

"I have studied the Old Law of Selath pertaining to challenges by combat. The minimum required for a victory by either participant is the drawing of blood with the blade. Though I am obliged to state that death of either participant will satisfy the conditions of the challenge, resulting in the other one being declared the winner. Have I interpreted correctly, Lord Osran?"

"You have, my lord. Though I wish to add that I have no desire to see your son killed this day, and I trust my son will honour this." He looked at Tonas, who nodded in respect to his father before turning to face Firrus.

"I have no wish to kill you, my lord. Please don't make me do so."

"You speak with confidence, my lord Tonas. Worry about yourself first." Firrus replied with a smirk.

Ainnarus raised his hand, then dropped it. "BEGIN!"

No sooner had the words left his lips than Firrus leapt forward with a flurry of thrusts, forcing Tonas onto the back foot. He wasn't used to fighting with a rapier, preferring a more traditional longsword instead. As such, he was used to less subtle parrying and more dodging.

As Yanara watched, she realized it was working to his advantage. Whenever he dodged, it forced Firrus to overextend and left him open to a counterattack. As fast as he was, Firrus seemed unable to adapt his duelling style to combat this difference.

The minutes passed, and Firrus began to tire. As he went in for another thrust, Tonas was ready for him. He stepped to the right, allowing Firrus' blade to sail dangerously close to his left side. As Firrus stepped in line with him, Tonas made a fist of his left hand and brought it down on the back of his opponent's head. At the same time, he wheeled around and traced the tip of his blade down across Firrus' back, cutting through to the skin underneath.

Yanara gasped as Firrus cried out in pain and dropped to his knees, rushing forward only to be stopped by Osran. "You will not interfere. Do not dishonour me further by flouting our laws." His voice was a growl, as though he was barely containing his anger towards her.

Composing herself, she watched as Tonas turned to Ainnarus and took a knee. "My lord, in accordance with the rules of the contest I have drawn blood. I trust this satisfies you?"

Yanara's heart sank. It was over. Firrus had been defeated, and their marriage would never be approved by Osran. The last few weeks disappeared in a well of her mind's despair, lost at the tip of Tonas' blade.

Maybe she could still disappear with Firrus? Go somewhere far away together, where Osran couldn't control her life? That had been her original plan.

"No." Firrus was clambering to his feet, his face contorted in pain from the wound on his back. A cold feeling crept over Yanara as he raised his rapier once more.

"The challenge is over, boy," Osran declared. "You lost, or does your honour mean nothing?"

"I will not give her up! She and I are meant to be together, and nobody will stand between us!" He roared the last words as he lunged forwards towards Tonas, his blade extended in front of him.

For a moment it seemed as though he had caught Tonas off guard.

Unfortunately, years of hunting had given Tonas sharp survival instincts, and he was not fighting in a contest now. He dodged instinctively, putting Firrus off balance again. As the blade passed his face, he grabbed Firrus' wrist with his left arm and pushed it away, leaning into him and thrusting his own blade up and through the young lord's ribcage.

Firrus stopped abruptly, his chin resting on Tonas' shoulder as he coughed blood. Tonas withdrew his blade, causing Firrus to drop his as he fell to his knees.

Yanara barely heard the scream leave her throat as she ran to Firrus. Tonas stumbled backwards, looking at his sister in horror as he realized what he had done. At the edge of the arena, Ainnarus cried out, his son Innis holding him in anguish.

Osran simply stood across from them, his arms folded across his chest in apparent indifference. Looking at him and Tonas, Yanara saw everything she hated in the world. A man who had denied her everything, and a brother who was the mirror of his father.

"Yanara," Firrus coughed, holding her hand in his. "Please, don't do anything stupid. You still have a whole life ahead of you. Perhaps my father will take you in. Perhaps…" And then he was gone, the end of his sentence a whisper on the wind.

An eternity passed before Yanara could even scream, and when she did it was one of abject pain and misery. Her scream echoed off the buildings around them and layered itself as though a chorus of widows were in the courtyard. She felt fire burning in her body, spreading up her spine and into her head. Collapsing onto the floor, she writhed in agony as the pain wracked her body. In her mind's eye, purple fire swirled in an endless maelstrom and a thousand faces recoiled in terror.

After what seemed like hours, the pain receded. Cold sweat clung to her skin, and her voice was hoarse from screaming. She clambered to her feet and looked around her. Both families were looking at her in terror, along with the many attendants who had come running at the sound of her screaming.

"Yanara," Tonas whispered with panic in his eyes, "your hair."

Looking down, her eyes widened at what she saw. Her gorgeous brown hair was now ice white from the roots to the tips. Pulling a mirror from her sidepouch with trembling fingers, she looked into it to see a stranger staring back at her. Even her eyebrows and eyelashes were white, as though she were some kind of albino.

Dropping the mirror onto Firrus' body, she looked at her father in panic. Osran stared back at her, his eyes wide with horror.

"Her hair," Ainnarus was saying from the other side of the courtyard. "I've heard the stories but…"

He trailed off, walking up to the body of his son and picking up the mirror. For a moment, Yanara thought he was going to return it to her, but he simply stepped away and handed it to an attendant.

"Osran, remove her from this place at once."

"Father?" Tonas asked. "What is it?"

"Didn't you know, boy?" Ainnarus interjected. "Your sister is a witch. She has the dark power of Mun."

What does he mean?

The last thing she saw before blacking out was Osran's face, regarding her with that familiar look of disdain. Or was it?

No.

That's pity. But why?

CHAPTER ELEVEN

THE MOON WAS still high in the night sky as Chessa awoke to frantic shouting and the sound of people running down the hallway outside her chamber. Ripping back the sheets, she leapt out of her bed and threw on her leather jerkin. She refused to sleep in normal bedclothes, and as such she already had on her breeches and undershirt. Strapping herself into her boots, she grabbed her sword and flung open the door into the hallway.

Her chamber was located at the entrance to the Houselord's wing, where Tonas and Ciloni now resided. It gave her easy access to their living space if needed, whilst allowing them some degree of privacy when not entertaining or dealing with House matters.

As she exited her chamber, she saw several Vasso guardsmen hurrying towards the guest wing and grabbed one of them as they passed. "Guardsman, what is happening?" she asked, fastening the sword belt around her waist.

"You need to come, Chessa," the man panted. "It's Naidar, the Talet lordling."

A sick feeling crept over Chessa as she ran with the man, shouting orders to other guards to secure various rooms and hallways. Relations between Houses Vasso and Talet were precarious, even with the success of the day's negotiations. If something had happened to the Talet heir, it would not go unanswered.

As they approached the hallway where Naidar and Javin had been accommodated, Chessa could see a commotion. Talet guards were blocking the entrance to Naidar's chamber and had been surrounded by Vasso guards. Both sides were armed, and it looked as though violence would ensue at any moment.

"Stand down!" Chessa ordered as she pushed her way through the Vasso guardsman. "Both sides, sheathe your swords!"

The Vasso guards immediately did as ordered, through several of them looked uneasy. They were highly trained by Chessa herself, and they had a bond which went beyond soldier and commander. The Talet guards remained where they were, however, and she rounded on them with fire in her eyes.

"You have drawn your weapons in another House. Under Selathi law, such an act is punishable by death. Now, I have ordered my men to stand down, which should prove to you that we are no threat. Will you let me pass at least?"

The Talet guards looked at each other nervously, before one spoke. "Just you, ma'am. The rest wait outside, though I must ask that you leave your weapon here with them."

She paused for a moment, looking at her sword. It didn't seem wise, but she had to get into that room. "As you wish," she replied. She removed her sword belt and handed it to one of her guards, exchanging a set of predetermined eye movements to let him know her intentions. The Talet guards moved aside and allowed her to enter the chamber.

What she saw inside made her heart sink.

Naidar was slumped against his bed with his throat slashed. Blood was congealing on his bedclothes, and his head was hanging lifeless. Javin stood over him, his eyes wide and his hands trembling. Yanara stood just behind the advisor, with one hand on his shoulder. She was quiet, her eyes surveying the scene before her, apparently quite shaken.

Chessa knelt by the young lord, examining his body but making sure not to touch him. Any trace of her on his corpse could be used as evidence to incriminate her. Naidar's face was chilling to behold, his eyes frozen open in terror. His skin was—

His skin was grey.

Not just pale, as one might expect from the shock of such a kill.

There was no colour, no blood in his cheeks. It was as though the life had been sucked from his very flesh, leaving behind an empty shell.

She carefully held the back of her hand up to his cheek. There was no residual heat emanating from his skin, as though he had been dead for hours.

Chessa stood and turned to Javin and Yanara. "My lord, my lady. When was he found?"

Javin attempted to answer, stuttering a few syllables. "A—about f—fifteen…" he muttered before falling silent again.

"He was found about fifteen minutes ago, Chessa," Yanara interjected, her hand still firmly on Javin's shoulder. "The guards heard a noise, presumably him falling against the bed, and after knocking with no answer they entered to find him like this."

Impossible, Chessa thought. His condition was that of a man who had been dead for hours, yet Yanara was implying he had died only fifteen minutes ago. "My lady, are you certain?"

"I am simply repeating what the guards told me, Chessa. Why?"

"His body is too far gone for him to have died so recently. His skin, his chill, all of it implies a death that took place hours ago at least."

Yanara's eyes narrowed for a moment, then returned to normal. She turned to Javin, still gripping his shoulder. "My lord, we must move him onto the bed. It is unseemly for him to be left like this."

Javin said nothing. His hands were clenched into fists, and he had begun to grind his teeth.

"My lord?" Yanara asked. "Javin? Did you hear me?"

"I hear you, *my lady*," he hissed. "Your family has done this, and now you feign compassion?"

Chessa blinked. Was the old man implying that House Vasso was responsible for assassinating the heir of House Talet?

Yanara tightened her grip on Javin's shoulder. "My lord, do you hear yourself? The idea that House Vasso could carry out such an act of violence is unthinkable. I could certainly never condone it."

"And what of your brother? Houselord Vasso's disdain for the young master was clearly visible during our talks. It would not surprise me to learn of his involvement in this barbarity," he snarled.

Chessa frowned. This was not the same Javin who had shown temperance and reason earlier that day. Something had happened to stoke his emotions, beyond the death of Naidar.

"I demand Houselord Vasso be brought before me at once!" Javin continued. "He must be made to account for himself this night!" He was becoming more agitated by the second, despite Yanara's attempts to calm him down.

As Chessa moved in to help her, her eye caught Yanara's for just a moment and she froze. There was something more there, beyond the usual cold gaze and latent dislike that Chessa usually got from her. She focused, desperately trying to figure out what she was seeing in that void behind Yanara's eyes.

As it came into focus, her breath caught in her throat.

Another eye, jet black and wreathed in purple fire stared back at her.

Suppressing a scream, Chessa stepped away and moved towards the door. Yanara looked at her, confused, before her eyes widened in horrified realisation.

An eternity passed between the two of them as they stared at each other, each waiting for the other to make the next move.

"Chessa," Yanara said dangerously. "Where have you been all night?"

You evil bitch.

"Asleep, in my chambers, *my lady.*"

"But nobody can vouch for that, can they Chessa?" Yanara's hand was now gripping Javin's shoulder so tightly that Chessa thought her nails might pierce his skin,

"You," Javin said with a growl as he looked at Chessa. "You acted on behalf of House Vasso to kill the young lord. You were only too pleased, especially after he insulted you this morning and caused a scene at the feast earlier."

This is bad. Things are about to get messy. If I'm right, there's no time to try and talk them down.

It was as though Chessa was moving without thinking about it as she broke for the door, smashing her elbow into the chest of the Talet guard on her right. As she emerged from the chamber, the Vasso guards took note of her movements and immediately separated to form a path through their ranks, drawing their swords. The guard she had handed her sword to was already throwing it to her as she shot through the gap, the guards closing ranks behind her.

"Cover me!" Chessa cried, as she reached up to snatch her sword out of the air. The sound of metal rung out behind her as guardsmen clashed, something she had hoped she would never hear within the walls of the keep. As she approached the end of the corridor adjoining the entrance hall, she distinctly heard Javin's voice.

"KILL THEM ALL! KILL HOUSE VASSO!"

The man was lost to madness and grief, spurred on by Yanara's twisted words. And what was that vision in her head? She shooked her head and pushed away the anxiety in her heart.

Crossing the entrance hall, Chessa considered that Yanara had responded to this turn of events far too readily for her to simply be taking advantage of the situation. She was ready for this, as though she had been planning it all along. Though it occurred to Chessa that a few Talet guards couldn't hope to bring down an entire House, even from within.

It was at that moment that the door to the keep crashed open and Talet soldiers poured into the hall, locking swords with the Vasso guards that were stationed inside. Chessa stopped and stared for a moment, stunned by what was unfolding before her.

Yanara *had* planned this.

There was no time now for pondering or delay. She had to get Tonas and his family to safety, before the Talets got their hands on them. As she drew her sword, a small number of Vasso guards caught up to her. Rallying them with a cry, she threw herself into the fray, deftly dispatching the Talet men as she cleared a path to the family chambers on the other side of the entrance hall.

I must keep my oath.

CHAPTER TWELVE

Fourteen years ago

IT HAD BEEN twelve hours since Firrus' death at the hands of her brother, and Yanara had only just stopped crying. Her throat ached, her eyes were red and her dress was covered in white hair which she had been pulling out in anguish and disbelief. At Ainnarus' insistence, she had been locked in a room in a far corner of the palace, away from her father and brother, and away from anyone who might see her.

A witch. That's what Ainnarus had called her. One who could use the power of something called Mun. What was it? How did she have that power? She was nineteen years old, and nothing like this had ever happened before. There had been no evidence to indicate she was anything other than a regular, unimpressive high born girl.

So what happened? Where did this come from?

A knock came on the door, making her jump. Brushing the hairs off her dress and wiping her eyes with a silk handkerchief, she cleared her throat.

"Come in," she said weakly, the words barely escaping her aching throat.

The door opened, and Osran stepped into the room, accompanied by two Akhani guards in their traditional black plate armour.

You. This is all your fault.

Osran turned to the guard. "Leave us."

They did not move.

"Do I have to repeat myself? Leave us, *now.*"

He growled the last word, causing the guards to exchange a quick glance before hurrying back out of the room. Turning back to Yanara, he walked over to the chair she was sat in, causing her to try and back away. But the chair was up against the wall, and she was stuck. He raised his hand, and she screwed up her eyes braced herself for another slap. None came however, and when she opened them again she saw Osran had pulled a long leather case from his back. Taking a knee, he placed it in front of her and opened it, revealing Firrus' rapier.

"In accordance with the rules of the contest, if either combatant dies then the other wins his weapon. Tonas was awarded Firrus' rapier by Ainnarus himself, but couldn't bring himself to keep it. So, he wants you to have it." Osran's voice was different. It was softer, without any of the usual gruff tones and haughty inflections she usually got from him. It was how she imagined a real father would speak to his daughter.

As she looked in his eyes, she saw the same pity she'd seen earlier. "What…what's happened to me?"

Her voice was barely a whisper, and Osran moved to touch her hand. She recoiled, however, and he respectfully withdrew to a chair on the other side of the table. "Ainnarus was right, Yanara. You are a Mun savant. You always have been."

"But I can't be. I mean, I have no powers, no memory of it. What's going on?"

Osran sighed, and Yanara saw a single tear rolling down his cheek. "Forgive me, my daughter. What I am about to tell you will be difficult to hear, but you must hear it now.

"When you were very little, perhaps only six years old, you told me one day that you knew I miss your mother. It wasn't just a general statement, either. You described, in detail, exactly why I missed her and what I thought about. You knew that when I looked at you I was reminded of her."

A memory of that day in the drawing room stung Yanara's heart.

"You told me that you could see images in my mind, including your mother. To me, a younger man, that was a terrifying prospect. So I took you to the capital, to be examined by the Vault Masters.

They confirmed that you did indeed have the abilities of a Mun savant, though they could not say for certain to what extent. Certainly you demonstrated the ability of MunSi, but there was no way to tell for certain if you would manifest any additional abilities."

Osran took a deep breath, and Yanara knew the real truth was coming.

"And so, in consultation with the men in that place, I took the decision to have your powers sealed along with your memory of them. The procedure caused you a great deal of pain, and it broke my heart to have to do it, but it was the right decision.

"The downside was that, as you have seen, intense emotional trauma could break the seal and return your powers and memories, along with other side effects. So I had to lie to you, Yanara. I could not hide my own guilt of what I had done to you, so I had to convince you that there was another reason for my behaviour towards you. If I could not, then you might well have discovered sooner what you really were and I was not prepared for that.

"So I chose to use your mother as the reason. I made you believe that you reminded me so much of her that I could not bear to have you around me. It was for your own good, but every time I pushed you away I died a little inside. And now here we are, in a land where the use of Mun is outlawed, and I wish I had you safely at home. I am so sorry, Yanara. You cannot know how sorry I am."

Yanara was in shock. Everything she had ever known was a lie. All the fights, the arguments, they had all been to distract her from the truth about who she really was. A life of misery and rejection, all to cover up powers that she didn't even know she had.

"Why?" she asked quietly.

"I told you, my daughter. To protect you."

"Protect me from what? You clearly convinced those men in the capital to do as you wished, so why couldn't you convince them to leave me alone altogether?"

"Not everyone is as open minded, Yanara. People would talk, would judge. You might even have been in danger."

"Who else knew that I had these abilities?" she asked, her voice rising.

"Ciloni and Moras were there that day, but only she saw what happened. I swore her to secrecy."

Ciloni knows!?

"She knows, and you made her keep it a secret!? Do you know how lonely I've felt all these years? Do you know what this has done to me?"

"I did it for you and for the family, Yanara."

There it was. The family. His reputation. The truth snapped into place like a bone being reset.

"This is about your relationship with Akhatar, isn't it? That's what it's always been about. They despise people like me, other savants, so for your own daughter to be one would put your precious relationship with them in jeopardy. I'm right, aren't I? AREN'T I!?" She screamed the last words, banging the table with her hand.

"Yanara, please. This hasn't been easy for me."

"Easy for you!?" She rose from the table and stood over him, the fire returning in her heart. "Just for once, try to think about someone other than yourself! You sealed my powers, treated me like an unwanted child for years, tormented me with your hatred and finally had your precious Tonas kill the man I loved!"

Osran sighed, and sat back in the chair. "A lot of things have happened that I regret, some more than others. But now is not the time for this. Ainnarus initially demanded that we leave immediately; however, I have managed to convince him to allow Tonas and I to stay for the sake of the trade talks. You, however, must return home at once."

He stood up and walked over to the door, opening it to let the two guards back in along with one of the attendants they had brought with them from Kyir.

"You will change into clothes more suitable to keeping a low profile, and then you will board a ship that I have charted to take you straight back to Kyir. You will disembark at Port Ainta and head home to Kyir from there. You will mention nothing of this to Moras, and there will be no discussion with Tonas or Ciloni. It's best we speak of this as little as possible."

He turned and regarded her for a moment.

"This is the safest course of action, Yanara. Once I return home, we'll talk again. I've missed you, my daughter."

And then he was gone.

* * *

THAT NIGHT, YANARA sat in the cabin of the ship that Osran had procured to take her safely back to Selathar. True to its name, the Tranquil Sea had been kind to them thus far, and she hadn't experienced much nausea.

Her attendant Irya was in the corner stitching some additional clothes for the journey now that Yanara was unable to use her dresses. The men of the boat had been paid not to ask questions, though Irya reported that she had heard some of them speculating.

Let them speculate. I don't care what they think.

Yanara was still struggling to come to terms with everything that had happened that day. Her life had been completely turned around, her heart was broken and she had a headache that threatened to knock her unconscious. She kept getting flashes of distant memories, possibly from when she was much younger but she found herself unable to make sense of them. If only Osran hadn't taken them away from her…

Osran. Everything that had happened in her life, everything that had gone wrong was because of him. His fear, his selfishness, all of it had caused her so much pain that she could barely contain herself.

Another memory flashed through her mind. Tied to a stone block, looking at the ceiling, with pain screaming through her body. Had that been the sealing of her powers?

Flash. Running in the garden, Osran picking her up with a look of love in his eyes.

She shook her head and tried to banish the memories, but they wouldn't go. All they were bringing now was pain, and she would give anything for things to go back to the way they were.

But she knew now. She knew the man her father really was. A liar, a coward and a thief. A liar for concealing the truth from her all these years and convincing her it was because of her mother that he hated her. A coward for being too afraid of what people thought to stand up for his only daughter. And a thief for stealing not only her childhood from her, but also a part of who she really was.

The nausea which had sat quietly in the pit of her stomach suddenly rose without warning, and she collapsed to the floor, vomit spattering onto the deck. Irya gasped and ran over with a cloth. "My lady, are you alright?"

"Do I look alright, Irya? Fetch the doctor, please."

"Right away, my lady." She rushed out of the cabin, leaving Yanara by herself.

Most ships this size didn't carry doctors, but Osran had insisted on having one board the ship in case anything happened to Yanara and had paid a substantial amount of money to convince the doctor currently with them to sail to Ainta and back.

Irya reappeared in short order with the doctor and a basin of water.

"Spot of seasickness, my lady?" the doctor asked, feeling her forehead with the back of his hand. "No, no that's not it. Have you felt sick this whole time?"

"No, it happened just now, without warning."

Helping her back onto the chair, the doctor gently felt her stomach with his hand. Frowning, he looked her in the eyes. "I'm going to ask you a question now, my lady. Please do not be embarrassed, but how long has it been since you bled?"

Suppressing a momentary feeling of outrage, Yanara considered how long it had been. "Actually…it's been about six weeks. Why?"

Wait. No. Please, no.

"You don't mean…"

"I'll need to do some more tests, but these are symptoms that generally accompany the early stages of your condition. I believe you may be pregnant, my lady."

CHAPTER THIRTEEN

BREAKING FREE OF the melee that had consumed the entrance hall, Chessa rushed up the steps to the hallway that led to the family chambers. What she saw ahead of her made her heart sink.

The door to the Houselord's chambers had been smashed in, and she could hear fighting coming from within.

Tonas. Ciloni!

Sprinting down the hallway, she saw Deran leaving his chambers with a sword in hand. "Chessa, what on earth is happening?!" he demanded.

"No time," she said, pushing him back into the room. "We have been betrayed, my lord. Yanara has turned the Talets against us. Get the children dressed and go to the library." There was a hidden passage in there, one that Chessa had truly believed they would never have to use. "I will find your parents and join you. Go!"

She pulled the door shut and turned to proceed down the hallway towards Tonas' chambers but was greeted by the sight of four Talet soldiers pouring in through a side door.

"Talet dogs!" she shouted at them, distracting them from the fight inside the chamber. They moved towards her with swords drawn, clearly confident that they could overpower a single woman.

She slowly walked towards them, blood dripping off the end of her sword and hitting the floor. Taking a deep breath, she adopted a defensive stance and locked eyes with the lead man. "Come, dog. Die in the name of your treacherous lord."

That insult was enough to goad the man into rushing her, and she side stepped his lunge with ease. As he passed her, she spun around and swung her sword with enough force to slice through the top of his spine. As she followed the spin through to face the remaining three men, the man dropped to the ground behind her to lay lifeless on the floor, blood seeping into the carpet runner.

The others charged as a group, probably thinking that numbers would give them an advantage. But they were not trained to work as a team like her own hunters, and they were unable to time their attacks to take advantage of gaps in her defence. She moved amongst them with ease, inflicting crippling cuts on them and dispatching each as they dropped their guard.

As she thrust her sword through the neck of the last man, she looked into the room at the end of the corridor to see Tonas slicing the throat of another guard in his chamber, before stumbling backwards onto his bed with blood soaking through his robes. Chessa wrenched her sword from the body of the guard, and dashed down the hallway.

Bursting into the room, the scene before her was like one from a nightmare. Broken furniture was scattered about the room, along with the bodies of several Vasso and Talet guards. Blood was soaking into the rug at the foot of the bed, upon which laid Tonas and Ciloni.

Ciloni had been disembowelled, and her body was sprawled on the bed with her eyes wide open. Tonas sat against the head of the bed, tears running down his face and the blood stain on his stomach growing bigger by the second. He cradled Ciloni's body in his arms, his tears falling onto her face as he wept.

Chessa suppressed the nausea rising in her stomach and stepped up to the bed. "My lord, forgive me. I have failed my oath to you. I was not able to protect you, and now this has happened."

"Chessa," Tonas said with a whisper, "please. You could not have foreseen this. Neither of us could have known what Yanara was capable of."

Shocked, Chessa simply stared at him.

"I sense she is responsible." He coughed, blood dribbling down his chin. "I've felt something was wrong all day, and this could not have happened without her scheming. But there is no time now for speculation or debate. You must take Deran and the children to safety. Yanara will not allow them to live and challenge her for the line of succession. Your oath stands whilst they remain alive. Please, you must save them at all costs."

"You may yet live, my lord."

"Perhaps. But I will only slow you down, and if you try to take me then we will all die for certain. Besides, I knew this day would come. I've known it ever since that fateful day in Akhatar when I killed the man she loved. I didn't mean for it to happen, but it happened. And she is right to hate me. But her hatred will destroy this house and destabilise the entire region. You must stop her. Here."

Chessa gasped as he handed her his sword. It was a beautiful blade, with an ornate gold handle. "I cannot take this, my lord."

"You can, and you will. Or must I make it a command?"

Just like your wife. So stubborn.

As a single tear rolled down her cheek, Chessa nodded. "As you command, my lord. I swear I will get the rest of your family to safety."

"Thank you, Chessa."

Tonas closed his eyes and rested his cheek on Ciloni's head. Tearing herself away from the bed, Chessa strode towards the door without looking back. She would take Deran and the twins someplace safe. She would kill anyone who got in her way.

She would return to Vasso Keep one last time.

And kill the woman who had torn their lives apart.

CHAPTER FOURTEEN

Thirteen years ago

YANARA LOOKED ON with dispassionate eyes as the caravan appeared slowly over the horizon, the flags of House Vasso fluttering from the carriages in the morning breeze. There were three in total, one for Osran, one for Tonas, and another for the attendants. She knew it was them; her attendant maid had delivered the news of their impending arrival the night before.

Seven months had passed since Firrus' murder at the hands of her brother in Laktam. The voyage back had been rough, mostly due to her morning sickness but also due to the memories that returned to her daily. The events back in Akhatar had broken her spirit, and she knew that the girl she had once been was long dead.

Her powers had returned as well, though she had kept that fact a closely guarded secret. It had started slowly, sensing the thoughts and feelings of the servants from time to time. She had quickly learned not to react to those emotions, lest the individuals figure out what she was doing.

As the weeks and months had passed, she had experimented to see what the extent of her powers were. Spending time in the library, her research on Mun and its different powers had taught her much that Osran would never have allowed. She knew she could read emotions, known more commonly as MunSi but the more she read and the more she pushed herself she realised that other abilities were at her command. Each exacted a harsh toll, and so she promised herself that she would not use them unless absolutely necessary.

Since her return, she had refused to leave the Keep. The servants whispered of her brooding, as though she couldn't hear them outside her chambers. The only person she interacted with for any length of time was Moras, who had struggled to balance his concern for his sister and his loyalty to their father.

That struggle had placed a strain on their relationship, and as the months went by she felt him slipping away from her, until he barely came to visit her at all. It hurt, but she was used to it by now. Everyone she thought she cared about was taken from her, leaving her with nothing. Except…

A soft knock came on the door, and her maid entered with a tray. "Your breakfast, my lady," she said with a bow.

Yanara said nothing, continuing to look out of the window. She heard the maid place the tray down and leave the room, closing the door behind her. As the girl left, Yanara almost thought she could sense fear from her.

She had long since stopped going to the dining room to eat, and now took her meals in her chambers. She was tired of observing protocol, of waiting to be served meals, of worrying about using the wrong cutlery for the wrong dishes in front of judgemental eyes. None of it mattered to her anymore.

Since her childhood, she had fought day and night for approval from her father and her brothers. Every time she thought she was getting close to be considered a true member of the family, something happened to snatch that dream away. The harder she fought, the harder it was when she failed.

Osran had persecuted her for something which was beyond her control, and when she had tried to break free and release him from his apparent misery, he refused to let her go. Why did he keep her tied to him when she clearly caused him such pain?

Tonas wasn't much better. He spent all his time worrying about what Osran thought of him and had never had much time for her. He echoed Osran's lessons to her at every opportunity like a damned parrot, and she was sick of it.

She wouldn't take their latent abuse anymore. Osran had denied her his love, and now Tonas had denied her a husband. She was done with allowing those two men to exercise control over every aspect of her life.

But what of Moras? He'd always been good to her, hadn't he?

A cold resolve settled in her mind. He could have been better.

* * *

IT WAS JUST before noon when another knock came on the door, this time firmer and more deliberate. Yanara was sat by the window reading and chose to ignore it. The knock came again, and Moras' voice sounded from the other side of the door. "You can ignore me all you like, but I know you're in there."

She rolled her eyes and placed the book down beside her. "Come then," she said dryly.

The door opened gently and Moras entered, his face solemn. Closing the door behind him, he walked over to the bed and sat down on the edge, brushing out the creases that appeared.

"We missed you this morning," he said softly.

"Don't lie, Moras, it doesn't become you," Yanara said sharply.

"Fine, I missed you. I know we don't speak much anymore, but you're still my sister." There was a sadness in his voice, as though he were resigned to some miserable inevitability.

"So, what about the elder Vassos?" she asked, allowing her resentment to filter into her voice.

Moras fidgeted nervously, looking at the floor.

"Moras?"

He looked at her, pity in his eyes. "After Father sent you home, he and Tonas stayed in Laktam for another two weeks trying to salvage the trade agreements they'd been working out before…the incident. They tried every deal they could think of, but Ainnarus just wasn't the same after that. His son Innis tried to take over, but he's not a competent negotiator."

"Did Ainnarus blame Tonas for what happened?" She tried to push away her pain at the memory of that day.

"He didn't blame anyone. Not Tonas, not Firrus, not even you. According to Tonas he just…stopped being himself."

"What do you mean?" Yanara asked, a puzzled look on her face.

"He just couldn't muster the strength for anything. Apparently he's a shadow of what he was. Innis has been forced to take over most of the daily work involved in running Laktam. Ainnarus is still the regent, but he's no longer fit to rule."

Yanara felt sorry for him. Everything she had witnessed of Ainnarus in the time they had been there indicated he was a loving, decent father, and a wise leader. He hadn't deserved to be a victim of the fallout that day. "So they stayed for two weeks and…then what? Just gave up? Where have they been since?"

Moras had a dark look on his face, and she knew this was a conversation he wasn't looking forward to. "In the Capital, Yanara. They spent the rest of the time in Selossa."

"Why?" she asked, her mood darkening.

"I wish I didn't have to be the one to tell you this," Moras said tentatively.

"Oh, just get on with it!" Yanara's patience was running out.

"Father has made a petition to the Arch Patriarch. He has asked…that you be banned from ever marrying."

Yanara stared at him in disbelief.

Banned from marrying? What does that accomplish?

"Why? What does he have to gain from me being a lonely old spinster for the rest of my life?"

"He didn't tell me why," Moras replied, shrugging, "only that I had to deliver the message. I'm sorry."

She got up from the bench and poured herself a cup of wine. "Don't apologise. You only did as you were asked, as always."

"What's that supposed to you mean?"

"It means, Moras," she snarled, rounding on him, "is that you've always been a snivelling, grovelling little sycophant who's only ever been worried about pleasing that vile old man. Only you've always been in Tonas' shadow, so you can never be the favourite son. You're stuck between your desire to be recognised by Osran and your jealousy of me because I don't pander to his arrogance."

Moras' face was one of absolute heartbreak, and for a moment he looked like he was about to cry. Stunned by her own words, Yanara turned away from him and took a moment to compose herself. She couldn't allow anyone to see her as weak, not even Moras. She made a noise of revulsion and sat back down. "Get out. You're infecting my chamber with your pathetic behaviour."

Biting his lip, Moras moved towards the door. Before he left, he turned to look at Yanara. "You know, just now when you were being a bitch? You sounded just like him," he said with tears in his eyes. He turned and left, pulling the door shut behind him.

She listened as the sound of his footsteps faded away, maintaining her composure as long as she could before bursting into tears. She hadn't intended to hurt Moras, and she certainly didn't mean what she said.

Or did she?

She *had* sensed those feelings from Moras. She'd never known before, but with the return of her abilities she knew how he felt. She knew he loved her in his own way.

It didn't matter now. She'd ruined her relationship with him, the last of her family. Nobody else remained now.

Well, except for her.

Finishing her wine, she placed the goblet back on the tray, and walked round to the side of her bed. There, next to the side table, sat a beautiful wooden crib decorated with gold leaf.

Inside the crib lay a sleeping infant girl, with jet black hair and delicate porcelain skin. Yanara gently stroked her cheek, looking lovingly at the tiny child who was now the centre of her world.

"It's just me and you now, my love. Nobody else matters, my darling Sima."

This tiny human, asleep in front of her, was the last reminder she had of the man she loved. The man taken away from her by Osran and Tonas. In that moment, she vowed that one day she would visit pain upon them in equal measure to that she had suffered.

For now, she would watch. And wait.

CHAPTER FIFTEEN

CHESSA SLOWLY OPENED the door from Deran's chambers, listening for approaching Talet soldiers. Hearing nothing, she put her eye in line with the crack in the door to see if she could spot anyone in the hallway. It was bizarrely quiet, though she could hear combat elsewhere in the keep. Had the Talet soldiers moved on already? And if so, why had they done so without checking the room they had been hiding in?

"Chessa, what on earth is happening?" Deran had a frantic expression on his face, and he was clutching the twins to him fiercely.

"My lord, as I said before there is no time. We must leave."

"No Chessa, you need to explain it to me. Now."

She sighed. Whilst a kind and generally open-minded man, Deran could be stubborn when he chose to be. If he was insisting on an explanation, then he would refuse to go anywhere until she gave him one. "Naidar Talet is dead, my lord. Murdered in his chamber, though I cannot say who the assassin was."

"How is this possible?" Deran had a stunned expression on his face. "And what was that you said about Yanara betraying us?"

Chessa sighed, knowing that what she was about to say would be hard to believe. "She was twisting Javin's mind, stoking his grief at the loss of his lord. Maybe she drugged him with something, I don't know. But it's clear she's been ready for this for a long time."

Deran slumped into a chair, lost for words. The twins, usually so confident and vocal, remained silent as they held each other's hands. "It can't be. She's always been at odds with Father and Lord Osran, but surely she wouldn't go this far? She organised the talks, she encouraged this agreement between our Houses. What does she have to gain from it?"

"If I had to venture a guess, I would say she wants your line dead, my lord. She's demonstrated time and time and again that her only real loyalty is to herself and her daughter. Given her feelings and talent with wordplay, it is likely that she will deflect any anger towards herself and focus the Talet retribution solely upon your father's line."

Deran's head shot up in panic. "We need to find Father and Mother! They won't stand a chance against the Talets!" Leaping up from the chair, he made for the door but Chessa was already holding him back. "Let me go, Chessa! We have to save them!"

"It's too late! There's nothing we can do for them!"

"You don't know that!" Deran fought against Chessa's strong arms.

"Yes I do!" she retorted, tears in her eyes as her voice softened. "Yes, I do."

Deran stopped struggling, realisation dawning on him as he looked into her face. "Chessa?"

She released him, wiping the tears from her face with a sleeve. "The Talet soldiers. They got to your parents before I was even close to their chambers. I am so sorry, my lord. My little ones. Please forgive me."

Deran fell to his knees, the twins rushing to his arms. They buried their little faces in his shoulders, their hands clutching at his shirt as he wrapped his arms around them. The three of them simply knelt on the floor for a time, quietly sobbing as Chessa watched them with a heavy heart.

Eventually they broke away, their eyes red from crying. Chessa took a knee in front of Deran, and placed a hand on his shoulder. "My lord, listen to me. Yanara has planned all of this, right from the start. She was ready to plunge this House into chaos and death well before Naidar died. His death was simply the opportunity she had been waiting for."

Deran looked at her, quietly sniffing. "Are you saying she killed him?"

Chessa frowned. Whilst Yanara was many things, she was not a violent woman. She had always found such things distasteful, especially after the events in Laktam. In Naidar's chambers, she had seemed troubled. Was that just part of her act? Or had she truly been surprised by his death?

Yanara must have made a deal with House Talet to use their troops to supplant Tonas' line and install her as the Houselord Vasso. With her in the seat, she could have promised House Talet anything, made any deal she desired. Chessa wasn't sure if Yanara's manipulation of Javin was part of her initial plan, but it had definitely produced the same result.

But then, who had killed Naidar?

"I do not know who killed him, my lord, but I do not think it was Yanara. My suspicion is that he was part of her plan to seize control of the House, which would explain why there are so many Talet soldiers, but when he died she had to improvise. Javin's reaction to Naidar's death was far more emotional than I would expect from him, given his position and demeanour. She was pushing him into conflict."

Deran hung his head in despair. "So what do we do?" he asked quietly, his voice almost breaking.

Chessa placed her fingers under his chin and lifted his head until his eyes met hers. "My lord, I failed your parents. It was my duty to protect them, and I failed. But I am sworn to the Houselord Vasso, and right now that title legitimately falls to you. Even were it not so, I would protect you and the children with my life. I will see you to safety, you have my word."

At that moment, they heard shouting in the distance. Gesturing for Deran and the twins to remain where they were, Chessa cautiously opened the door and stepped into the hallway, sword at the ready.

She found herself alone, though judging by the noises coming from the other end of the hallway that was unlikely to be the case for very long. The library was in that direction, next to the Houselord's wing, which meant they were taking a serious risk of being caught by trying to make it to the escape passage.

It was, however, the only option left to them. If they remained, the Talet soldiers would not hesitate to kill them on sight. Even the twins wouldn't be safe, given Javin's emotional orders to his men.

Ducking back into the room, Chessa summoned Deran and the twins to her side.

"Listen to me carefully. We have to head straight for the library, as quickly and as quietly as we can. That means no talking, no gasping, no sound of any kind." She eyed the twins. "Do the two of you understand that?"

They nodded their heads vigorously, fear creeping onto their little faces. Smiling at them, Chessa turned to Deran and placed her hand on his shoulder.

"If we are spotted, I will cover your escape. The passage will take you out of the town where a carriage driver will be waiting to take you to Tuam. The Talet soldiers will be expecting any survivors to go straight to the capital, so by diverting to Tuam first you can avoid them on the roads from here to Selossa."

Deran had a troubled look on his face. "Chessa, you know Yanara won't leave it at this. As long as the children and I live, we're a threat to her and she knows it."

"Which is why we have to get you to Selossa. If we can make it that far, the Senate can protect you and see that Yanara is brought to justice. But first, we have to get out of the Keep."

Chessa stood and adjusted her jerkin, before strapping her sword belt to her waist. "Are you ready?" she asked, looking at the three Vassos. They nodded their heads, and she saw them visibly straighten up. She smiled, and turned to the door. "Then let's go," she said boldly.

Opening the door once more, she led them into the hallway. There were visible signs of struggle, amongst broken ornaments and torn carpet. As they proceeded towards the library, they could hear movement from within the Houselord's wing. Chessa looked at the others and mouthed for them to hurry, quickening her pace towards the library door.

As they reached the door, Chessa looked up at the door to Tonas' chambers and froze.

A pair of Talet soldiers was heading towards them, and there was not enough time to get Deran and the twins into the library before they were spotted.

She darted forward and pushed the door open, pushing the twins through. Vishki tripped and let out a cry, which drew the attention of the soldiers.

"You there, stop where you are!" The lead soldier drew his sword and broke into a run, his comrade following in quick succession.

Chessa went to grab Deran and push him into the library as she had with the children, but as she did so he grabbed her first and spun them on the spot. She was now between him and the doorway, and she knew what he was about to do. "My lord, you can't! My duty is to protect you, not the other way round!"

"I'm not completely helpless, Chessa."

And he rushed the men, swinging his sword wildly.

He was not nearly as competent as his father, but he did manage to land several blows that surprised Chessa. Unfortunately, he was not skilled in defence and took a number of cuts that caused him to cry out. The sound drew the twins back to the door, which Chessa slammed shut in their faces.

Eventually the soldiers began to tire, their armour weighing them down. As Deran dispatched the two of them, Chessa saw a figure in the doorway of Tonas' chambers, and her heart sank.

Yanara stood watching them, rapier in hand.

"Well, look what we have here," she said with a wicked smile. "Failing in your duties as a bodyguard, Chessa? I thought your responsibility was to protect the Houselord, not let him fight your battles for you."

Chessa stepped forward, letting go of the door handle. Deran stopped her and pushed her back to the doorway, which was now open behind her. "My lord, please don't do this," she pleaded as tears filled her eyes yet again. "I can't lose you, Deran."

Deran took her face in his hands and planted a gentle kiss on her lips. As he did, Chessa felt him press an object into her hand. She looked down as he pulled away, and saw the Kyir Emerald in her hand, the pendant of House Vasso that was worn by the heir. "You've been more than just a bodyguard, Chessa. You've been a friend to me, and the closest thing to a mother the children could have hoped for since Giva's death. But now I need you to let me go and get my children to safety."

Chessa nodded, tears staining her cheeks.

Deran smiled. "You're not the only one fighting for those you love today," he said before stepping back and pushing her through the doorway.

* * *

DERAN TURNED TO face his aunt, gripping his sword tightly.

"You're looking tired, aunt. Perhaps you should return to your chambers until the fighting is over."

Yanara laughed. "Spare me your clichés, boy. I'm done playing these stupid games. Everyone in this place is working to my design, to my plans. If you think you can save your pathetic children and that bitch lover of yours by challenging me, then I'm afraid you really haven't been paying enough attention."

The rapier in her hand twitched, and Tonas raised his sword in defence as Yanara leapt for him.

* * *

CHESSA SLAMMED THE door shut, her eyes still streaming with tears, and began to push a wooden bureau across in front of it. The twins ran forward, trying to stop her.

"You can't!" screamed Vishki, pulling at Chessa's arm. "Father won't be able to follow us!"

Corin was on the other side, trying desperately to push the bureau back the other way. "No!" he grunted, his little feet slipping on the floor.

Chessa grabbed them both and pushed them away as the muffled sound of fighting in the corridor rang in their ears. She pushed the bureau into place, before grabbing the twins as they attempted to run back to the door, their cries breaking her heart. "Listen to me, both of you! It's just us now, you hear me? I know you can't understand this now, but believe me you will. We need to leave, before those soldiers get in here and finish their job. Leave that bureau where it is and come help me."

Still sobbing, the twins followed her to the hearth where she reached up into the chimney and pulled out a bundle wrapped in cloth. Inside were some cloaks, including two small ones which she removed and placed over the twins' shoulders.

"You cannot be recognised on the outside, or this will all be for nothing," she said, throwing another cloak around herself and pocketing the Kyir Emerald. "Come, we must leave."

She reached back into the hearth and pulled a hidden lever, causing the back of the hearth to slide away revealing a dark passage just large enough for an adult to squeeze through.

Vishki sniffed and looked up at her. "Will we ever come back, Chessa?"

She looked down at the girl and smiled, before gently ushering them into the passage. As she followed them in, she pulled the lever again and allowed the back of the hearth to slide into place once more. "That will be up to you, my child."

And with that they disappeared into the darkness.

* * *

DERAN TRIED TO shut out the ringing of steel in his ears as he desperately tried to parry Yanara's rapid flurries. He had no idea when she had learned how to fight with a rapier, but she was good. She constantly kept him off balance, and every time he recovered she leapt back, forcing him to come to her.

"Why!?" he screamed at her, suddenly consumed by rage. "Why do this!? My children and I are innocent. We didn't kill your lover!"

Yanara laughed again. "You think I care about guilt?" she asked, unleashing another flurry of thrusts, scoring a hit on his left shoulder. The cut stung, and he tried to ignore it. "I'm beyond that now," she continued. "The only thing that matters in my life is my daughter. Everyone else is irrelevant, and anyone who isn't on my side is a threat."

That rage again. Deran lunged for her desperately, but she stepped to the side and lightly flicked her rapier across his back, spraying blood onto the ceiling. He collapsed into the wall, and turned to face her, leaning against the stonework.

"Stupid boy. I've survived more than you have ever had to face. Even the death of that miserable wife of yours didn't compare to the pain I've suffered."

The mention of Giva was too much for Deran to bear. Fury flooding his heart, he raised his sword over his head and charged Yanara with a scream. Emotion had compromised him, however, and as he drew closer he saw Yanara raise her rapier to him.

The tip pierced his throat and erupted from the back of his neck. The sword dropped from his hands and clattered to the floor behind him.

As Yanara wrenched the rapier from his flesh, he clasped his hand to his throat and blood began to gush through his fingers. The strength leaving his body, he collapsed to the ground with Yanara left standing over him.

"Oh nephew," she said with that silky voice she used when she was winning. "You look surprised. But you shouldn't be."

She took a knee next to him and whispered in his ear.

"After all, do you really think you're the first of our blood to die by my hand?"

CHAPTER SIXTEEN

Three years ago

YANARA OBSERVED AS the two stretchers were carried through the doors of Vasso Keep and towards the infirmary, frantic shouting echoing through the entrance hall. Each was borne by four guardsmen, their brows covered in beads of sweat from the strain of carrying a man in full hunting armour.

Emerging from the hallway where his chamber resided, Tonas ran towards the group with panic on his face. *Unusual for him*, Yanara thought. Like Osran, he was fairly apathetic these days, though he seemed to allow himself some measure of affection for his sons.

"What happened?" Tonas asked. "Moras! Kalim!"

Watching from the doorway of the Great Hall as her brother was pulled away from the guards by Chessa, the Companion Hunter, Yanara considered her for a moment. The woman had held the prestigious role for two years now, and she was still a mystery to Yanara. Her MunSi ability should have allowed her to read Chessa's emotions, giving her some insight into how the woman worked.

It had not.

The first time she had failed to read her, Yanara had assumed that she herself was the problem. That perhaps she was having an off day, or maybe it was down to her cycle. Her hormones had gotten in the way in the past, though she usually managed to get at least a flicker from the individual.

Perhaps it had something to do with Chessa's Lharasan heritage. She had heard tales of the people from the north having a peculiar resistance to the power of Mun. Some said it was a side effect of their harsh environment, others posed that it was their proximity to the unstable magical remnants of the Shattered Kingdom.

Regardless, the fact remained that she was unable to see the woman's intent, and that made her dangerous. The only thing Yanara knew about her for sure was that she was an unstable element in her plans, one that needed correcting.

That could wait, however. At present, there was another stray thread that needed cutting.

* * *

TONAS WEPT ALONE at the side of his eldest son's bed, his head bowed in grief. His tears ran down his cheek and fell softly to the stone floor, the sound echoing quietly through the room.

Kalim had been found in the forests south of Kyir, along with Moras. The two had been on a hunting trip, and against Tonas' better judgement Moras had refused to take an escort. When they hadn't returned the next day, Tonas had ordered the Hunters to scour the woodlands for the two of them until they were found. And found them they had, horrifically wounded and close to death. The search party had also found a boar nearby with blood on its tusks, indicating that it had been a tragic accident.

Upon returning to Kyir, the chirurgeon had managed to save Moras, but Kalim's condition had been too severe. Despite removing the tusk splinters that were embedded in his chest, he had lost too much blood. By the time his wounds were sewn up, there was nothing that could be done for him.

And so it was that Kalim Vasso, the firstborn son of Tonas and second in line to the Lordship of the House had passed away before his time, leaving his younger brother Deran as Tonas' sole heir.

It occurred to Tonas that their House was beginning to fall apart, slowly but surely. The schism between Yanara and Osran, the tragic breakdown of the Akhani trade talks eight years previously, and now the death of his own firstborn son.

No House should have to endure this much pain, he thought to himself.

Was it just misfortune, or was some other force at work here?

He shook his head. There wasn't time for superstitious nonsense, not now. Deran must be schooled to take his brother's place as heir, but by who? Tonas had never been a good teacher, and Katyana was busy instructing Sima, Yanara's bastard daughter.

Perhaps Moras, with his cheerful outlook and gentle spirit, would be a good teacher for him.

If he ever awoke from his sleep.

* * *

MORAS OPENED HIS eyes. They were heavy, like someone was pulling down on them. His throat was dry, and his chest ached. He was laid in his bed, cocooned in the sheets like an insect.

What the hell happened to me?

"Welcome back, brother." Yanara's voice came from the side of the bed, and he turned to look at her.

"Sister," he said weakly. "What happened?"

"You had an accident. It appears a wild boar didn't take kindly to your attempts to bring him home for dinner." She looked him dead in the eye. "I'm afraid Kalim didn't survive."

Moras felt a stab of grief, and tears filled his eyes. Kalim had been very close to him, almost like his own son. The hunt had been the boy's idea, and Moras had been surprised when Kalim had asked him to accompany him.

Hunting had never been Moras' strength, but Kalim was a promising hunter. It would have made sense to take one of the House Hunters with him, even Chessa herself.

But Kalim had asked Moras, asking him not to allow anyone else to join them. He had wanted to spend time alone with his uncle, and Moras could not refuse him. He loved his nephew and would have done anything for him.

And now he was dead. If Moras had been stronger, better at fighting, maybe he could have killed the beast and saved his nephew. He would have rather died himself if it meant saving Kalim's life.

"What about Tonas?" he asked, looking at Yanara.

"Understandably grief stricken," she replied. "Though I am given to understand he is already putting plans in place to prepare Deran to become the next heir."

Grief stricken. Because I failed to protect his son.

* * *

YANARA SENSED MORAS' guilt and smiled at him.

"He doesn't blame you if that's what worries you," she said quietly.

Not that he knows where the blame lies. One of the advantages of using someone else to do the killing.

She frowned as she saw Moras' eyes grow wide.

"What's wrong brother?" she asked nervously. It was as though he was realising something.

Moras was silent for a long time before he replied. "So, it was you. You're responsible for what happened to us."

Yanara froze, then forced a laugh. He couldn't possibly know. Could he? "That's absurd. I know we don't exactly get along these days but I'm hardly capable of orchestrating your deaths. Besides, what would I have to gain from it?"

"Everything. By slowly eliminating the rest of the family, you push the line of succession onto yourself and Sima. Even if you left me alive, you know I'll never have children and so you only have to wait for me to pass on and then it's all left to you. Of course, you'd have to make sure nobody suspected you, but then you know exactly what everything is thinking. Don't you, Yanara?"

A cold sweat began to break on her forehead. There was no way Moras could know about her gifts, unless Tonas had told him, but he himself had been sworn him to secrecy by Osran. "You're playing a very dangerous game right now, Moras. Perhaps you'd better get some rest."

"Don't toy with me, Yanara. Did you seriously think you were the only Mun savant in this family?"

Silence. Yanara was stunned. "You? YOU!?"

"Yes, me. For as long as I can remember. I was there when you demonstrated your abilities to Father all those years ago. Whilst you lived your life in blissful ignorance, I was forced to hide who I was or suffer the same fate. But then, I've gotten pretty good at that anyway. I've watched you grow up and tried to help guide your emotions, but I couldn't help you in Akhatar. And since you came back, you've been dark to me. I haven't been able to read you at all, and I 129ealized it's because your powers were blocking mine."

"Why didn't you stop Father?" Yanara asked, with tears welling up in her eyes. "You could have saved me."

"He would have done the same to me and you know it. But we're not talking about Father, we're talking about you, and what you've done. Why, Yanara? Why do this to all of us? There are innocent people in this family who have done nothing wrong!"

There are no truly innocent people in this family.

"It's too late. I've made my choice, as Osran and Tonas made theirs."

"You won't get away with this Yanara. They'll know if you stab or poison me now, or even smother me."

Wiping her eyes, she placed a hand on his chest. "Oh brother, you think I would use such crude weapons?"

* * *

MORAS INHALED SHARPLY as he felt a cold sensation wash across his chest. It was as though someone was pouring ice water across him, and his breaths grew short.

Looking down, he saw dark, inky purple smoke spreading from the point where Yanara's hand met his chest. Turning to look at her, he saw her eyes were jet black, like obsidian glass. Despite their inhuman appearance, he thought he could see sadness in them.

"Yanara," he groaned weakly, "what are you?"

"Shhh, brother," she whispered. "I am so sorry it's come to this."

She's using MunVa. She's mindflaying me.

He tried to reach for her, but the strength had all but gone from his body. The smoke enveloped him, leaving him numb. Tears in his eyes, he battled to get the words to leave his lips.

"Why?"

Then darkness took him.

* * *

YANARA RELAXED, ALLOWING the smoke to dissipate into the air. She fought back tears as she grappled with the reality of what she had just done.

She wished she could have saved him, above all others. He had always been kind to her, and they had been close once. But those days were over. The past five years had proved to Yanara that the only person she could really rely on was herself.

Nobody else could be trusted to act in the best interests of her or her daughter. Sima was everything to her now, something she'd never envisioned before, and she would do everything in her power to protect her. Sima was all she had left of Firrus, the very last reminder of the man she had loved above all others.

Her decision to have Moras and Kalim assassinated had been a hard but necessary one. Removing Kalim from the line of succession put more strain on Tonas and Deran, making them vulnerable.

As for Moras, it was a simple matter of resolve. The assassin's failure to kill him had given her the opportunity to test her commitment and her powers. She had the power of MunVa, the ability to burn away a person's mind, but it was not something to be done lightly. If she did it too much, her own emotions and mind would be at risk. Moras was an experiment.

After all, if she could find the strength to burn away everything he was, there was nothing she couldn't do.

CHAPTER SEVENTEEN

TWO DAYS HAD passed since Chessa and the twins had escaped from Vasso Keep following Yanara's betrayal. The carriage had indeed been waiting for them on the outskirts of Kyir as promised. Thankfully the Talet troops had been too few in number to form a perimeter around the town, and they had managed to slip away without being noticed.

The twins had been unusually quiet since their departure. Chessa had expected them to cry more, perhaps Corin more than Vishki. But there was nothing from them. They barely spoke, unless it was to say they were hungry or that they needed to use the latrine.

Chessa got more conversation out of the carriageman. An elderly man called Mossan with a dry sense of humour, his musings on life in the western towns had provided a welcome distraction from her own thoughts these past couple of days.

In the space of four days, Chessa had lost two Houselords that she had sworn oaths to, plus the man she loved and the woman she looked up to. In normal circumstances she considered that this would have been enough to tip her over the edge and into inescapable grief, but she had the twins to worry about. So long as she had them, she could focus her attention on getting to Selossa and keeping them safe.

They were currently on the south coast road that led to Parello.

From there, they would head up to Tuam and across the river to Selossa. So long as they continued to make good time, Chessa surmised that they would be in Selossa in about a week's time.

A horn sounded in the distance behind them.

Her heart pounding in her chest, Chessa looked around the side of the carriage to see where the sound had come from. In the distance, she could see a small number of horsemen bearing down on them. One carried a banner, and Chessa desperately strained her eyes to see what the sigil was.

Green reeds on a white field.

House Talet.

There was no chance of them outrunning horses in a carriage. Chessa looked at the twins in the back of the carriage. She was loath to leave them, but if she didn't then they would be in even more danger.

"Stop the carriage, Mossan. I'm getting off."

Nodding in obedience, Mossan reined in the horse until the carriage came to a stop. Jumping down from her seat in the front and securing a shawl to hide her hair, Chessa walked round to the back and threw a blanket to the twins.

"Get under that, and stay quiet."

"But…" Corin began to protest, but Vishki was already pulling the blanket over the top of them.

Turning to face the horsemen, Chessa placed a hand on the pommel of her sword. To unsheathe it early would be to invite trouble. Besides, she was quick enough on the draw not to be disadvantaged.

As the riders approached, one of them called out.

"Ho there! What business have you on this road, traveller?"

Chessa eyed them with a cold look. They didn't appear to be from the same group that ransacked the keep. "A curious question for a man of House Talet," she observed, her grip tightening around her pommel. "To my knowledge, this road is under the jurisdiction of Houses Vasso and Nura. What's your authority to question travellers here?"

"We carry the authority of Houselord Vasso, to find those responsible for murdering our lord Naidar in the halls of Vasso Keep."

"And why doesn't Lord Osran send his own men?"

That ought to throw them.

The men looked at each other, then back at Chessa.

"Lord Osran passed away four days ago," their leader replied. "Lady Yanara is now Houselord Vasso."

"But what of Lords Tonas and Deran?" Chessa asked, feigning a confused expression. Her jaw clenched at the suggestion that Yanara was now Houselord.

"They…"

The leader was interrupted by one of his men, who whispered something in his ear. He nodded, then continued. "We are not here to answer questions, but to ask them. What business does a Lharasan woman have this far from the Wastelands?"

Looking down, Chessa noticed a lock of her red hair had fallen out of the shawl.

Damn, they noticed my hair.

"Just trading, gentlemen. Nothing you'd be interested in."

"And how do you know what we'd be interested in?"

The situation was getting tense. If they decided to look in the carriage it was all over.

An arrow sailed over her head and struck the lead rider squarely between the eyes. Looking behind her, she saw Mossan with a bow in his hand already nocking a second arrow.

Well, that's one way to deal with them.

Drawing her sword, she ran towards the other riders as Mossan released another arrow, which caught one of the riders in the shoulder. He fell back off his horse in agony and hit the ground, where Chessa quickly rammed her sword through his heart. The other two riders had circled around and were now bearing down on her. They were riding in a pair, preparing to hit her from either side.

Time for something a little unorthodox.

She broke into a run towards them, her sword in her left hand. As she got close enough, she drew Tonas' sword from the sheathe on her back and dropped to her knees, skidding in the dirt. Swinging the swords either side of her, she slashed the legs of both horses and caused them to crumple behind her. The riders were thrown from their mounts, one landing on his head. He did not get back up.

The other rolled into the ditch, and slowly got to his feet with a groan. But Chessa was already upon him by the time he had reached for his sword, and the last thing the man saw was Tonas' sword swinging towards his face.

Breathing heavily, Chessa wiped down the swords and looked around her as she sheathed them. Four riders had found them, so soon as well. There would be more behind them, and it was reasonable to assume that the others would know to look for a Lharasan woman with two children.

Looking into the back of the carriage, she saw the twins peeking over the top of the blanket. For the first time in their lives, her presence was a threat to them. If she stayed with them, she would simply attract unnecessary attention.

Her heart sank as she realized what she had to do.

"Mossan, how long have you been using a bow for?"

"As long as I can remember, Lady Chessa."

"Good. I'm leaving the twins in your care. I have to go."

"But, Lady Chessa," he protested, "what about the children?"

"It's no longer safe for me to be with them, Mossan, and I have other things I need to deal with. Take them to Tuam and then onto Selossa. As fast as you can."

"Where will you go?"

"Back to Kyir. I've been running from unfinished business, and it's time I took care of it."

She clambered into the back and knelt beside the children.

"It's time for you to grow up, and fast," she said, pressing the Kyir Emerald into Vishki's hand. "This belongs to you two now. Look after it, and don't let anyone else see it except the Paragon in Selossa. Do you understand?"

With so much trauma and so much loss, the twins had no energy left to protest. They simply nodded and hugged her, then slumped back in the carriage and fell asleep.

"Take care of them, old man," Chessa said with a warm smile. "I'll be back for them one day, you hear?"

"Understood ma'am," Mossan said with a mock salute. "Take care of yourself now."

And with that, the carriage rattled off into the distance, the twins staring at her with pain in their eyes.

Pulling the shawl from her head and letting her deep red hair blow in the wind, Chessa looked back along the road towards Kyir and steeled herself for the trials to come.

She still had one more promise to keep.

CHAPTER EIGHTEEN

YANARA WATCHED AS the funeral procession came to a stop in the square outside the front of Vasso Keep. The townsfolk were crying, waving handkerchiefs and other symbols of their grief. Six coffins were hoisted into place on the funeral pyres that had been prepared the night before. A large number by all accounts, but especially when they were all from the same family.

Osran's funeral hadn't taken place when the Talets had arrived for the negotiations, so his body had been stored in the coolroom under the kitchen ready for his cremation. In addition to his coffin, there were those for Tonas, Ciloni and Deran.

There were also two smaller coffins for the twins. Of course, the townsfolk had no idea that they weren't actually inside, as Yanara's men had been unable to locate them or Chessa.

Taking stock of what had happened over the last few days, Yanara considered that it had all gone rather well. Not counting the twins, she had wiped the remainder of Osran's line from existence and secured her position as Houselord. In addition, the fool Naidar had been killed as well, though the cause of his death was still a mystery to her. Whilst pushing Javin over the edge of grief and rage, she had been unable to detect anything from the others who were there that day, and Chessa's evaluation of the body raised some interesting questions.

Those questions could wait, however. For now, she had to make her mark on Kyir and the other Houselords. If they sensed any weakness from her, they would surely move to have her supplanted by someone more agreeable to their own ambitions. Certainly, House Nura would not take kindly to having yet another Houselord Vasso who wasn't married to one of their own.

"What happens now, mother?" Sima's voice suddenly interrupted her thoughts.

She turned to look at her daughter, who was stood next to her. She was still shaken by what had happened, but she was a strong-willed girl. She would survive and grow to become a wonderful young woman thanks to the choices that Yanara had made. Choices with consequences which would continue to unfold as the days and weeks went on. "Now, it's just us my love. I am Houselord, and you are my heir. Terrible things have happened, but now you and I are free to make things the way we want them to be. Not even the actions of a rogue heir could harm us."

House Talet had all but absolved themselves of responsibility following the carnage a few days previously. Imdan himself had rode south to announce that his son had operated without his permission, something Yanara knew would be believed by the ignorant masses. Many of the Houselords would be skeptical, but they had no proof that Imdan was behind it. In addition, she herself had pardoned House Talet and allowed Imdan to remain for the funeral. The only other alternative was war, and that would simply undo all she had achieved in the last few days.

"Lady Yanara."

Imdan presently stepped up from behind her, his cool demeanour radiating from him like the sun. Yanara had a great deal of respect for the man, but there was something about him that unnerved her. "Lord Imdan. My condolences on the death of your son. I am sorry that you did not see fit to bury him here."

"He belongs in Manar."

That's strange. I sense no grief from him at all. No pain at the loss.

Yanara decided to dig a little deeper. "Had you allowed my chirurgeon to carry out an autopsy, we might have found out exactly how he died."

"Irrelevant. He is dead. The manner in which he died will not bring him back."

No curiosity over how he died. No desire to find out. Wait.

Yanara frowned, not looking away from the funeral pyres, which were now being lit.

He knows how it happened.

He arranged it.

Imdan had his own son killed.

Taking a deep breath, Yanara ran through the situation in her head. If Imdan had arranged for his son to be killed, that was a crime punishable by execution and even the stripping of his title. House Talet would be replaced by another House as the rulers of Manar.

Could she use this against him?

"You are correct, of course. Though, I imagine the Paragon might be interested to know how your son died. And if you can't provide an answer backed up by the Houselord who was there at the time, then he might start asking questions. Questions that I know the answer to."

Imdan looked at her, concern growing on his face. "What do you mean?"

She turned to him and stepped closer, so their faces were mere inches apart. "I know you killed him, Imdan," she whispered. "You know the punishment for that."

"How could you possibly know that?"

"Look into my eyes."

She watched as Imdan locked eyes with her, and recoiled slightly at what he saw. "You…you're one of them."

"Yes. I have done things you can't imagine, Imdan, but killing your own son? I can make that haunt you for a very long, long time."

The elder Houselord stepped back and considered her for a moment. "Go ahead. You will never be able to prove it. And if you do try to bring me down, I'll not only reveal your scheming with my son but also the existence of your twisted powers. If House Talet falls, so does House Vasso."

Yanara clenched her jaw, then softened her expression. "It appears we're on equal footing, my lord. On the one hand, we were both involved in allowing this plan to go ahead. However, each of us has our own secret, one that the other knows. Perhaps we can reach an agreement to keep what we know to ourselves? The chaos of war would ruin us both."

"Very well," Imdan replied, refusing to look at her. "You have my word, woman. But I don't take kindly to threats."

"Neither do I, Imdan. So long as we're on the same page, we'll be fine. Oh, and one more question. How *did* you kill Naidar?"

Imdan fixed her with a cold stare, then leant forward and whispered a word in her ear that made all the colour drain from her face. Her mind conjured up images of the stuff of nightmares, and she was overcome by uncontrollable trembling. As he pulled back he smiled at her, then turned back to face the funeral pyres.

Yanara watched light from the flames flicker over his face, showing the aged skin and deep creases. As she did, she realized that in spite of all the things she had done and all the sacrifices she had made, compared to her this man was a true monster.

The pyres burned slowly, releasing plumes of billowing smoke into the night sky. The only sounds to be heard were the crackling of the fires and the weeping of the people below.

House Vasso was reborn that night.

EPILOGUE

THE MORNING SUN reflected off the marble walls of Tuam's Azure District, illuminating the vast assembly of docks and wharfs scattered along the waterline. Dawngulls hung in the morning breeze, occasionally swooping down to pluck fish from the shallow water.

Vishki took a bite of the bread roll she was holding in her hand, watching the local urchins scurrying about the trader's cart, snatching what they could. Once upon a time, she would have judged them simply for being who they were, apathetic to their struggles.

Things were different now.

Five years had passed since their escape from Kyir after Yanara's betrayal and the subsequent massacre of their father and grandparents by House Talet. It had taken them some time to recover from that loss, especially after Chessa had left them in Mossan's care.

The plan had been to take them to Tuam and then on to Selossa, but without Chessa they had no idea where they should go when they got there. Neither did Mossan for that matter, and upon arriving in Tuam he had decided they would be safer staying there than going to Selossa where they would be more likely to run into members of House Talet. He had given them a few coins and then rather unceremoniously abandoned them before heading back to Kyir.

And so it was that the twins had spent five years living amongst the street urchins of Tuam, learning how to survive, hide and generally keep themselves out of trouble. It had been hard at first, but they had now been common children for almost as long as they'd been highborn.

"What you thinking, sis?" Corin asked in his common voice.

"Just stuff," she replied. "Thinking how we got here."

"By carriage, remember?"

"Shut up."

Corin chuckled, giving her a hug. They still teased each other, but their shared trauma had brought them closer than ever. "Shall we get to work, sis? Busy day ahead."

"Definitely," Vishki replied with a nod. Clambering to her feet, scanning the crowd for potential targets. She watched as a small boat approached the pier in front of them, and a young woman secured it to the pier before leaping out with a large sack slung over her shoulder. "And I think we've found our first target," she said, rubbing her hands. "Let's go."

Grinning at each other, the twins hopped down from their perch and headed into the bustling crowd, just as they had every morning for the past five years.

AFTERWORD

This afterword will seem a little strange, but it's something I wanted to get across to those who have just finished reading my first published story.

I am not a professional author. I've never tried or pretended to be. This is not my attempt to become the next Brandon Sanderson, George R.R. Martin, or J.K. Rowling. I simply want to tell my stories. I hope that those who wish to go on and review my little novella will bear that in mind - remember, in today's world, kindness matters above all else.

Printed in Poland
by Amazon Fulfillment
Poland Sp. z o.o., Wrocław

64016770R00081